"Are you afraid I'll compromise you if you stay
a moment longer under my roof?"

"There's not the slightest chance of that," she
snapped.

"No?" He stood so near she caught the male
scent of him and felt her knees go weak.

"Then perhaps it's this you're afraid of."

His head came down. His mouth found hers.
She struggled fiercely, but only for a moment.
The searching warmth of his lips, the insistent
manner in which his embrace molded her to him
set fire to her passions. Her need for him
betrayed her, and she discovered herself clinging to him with an ardor that appalled her, but
which at the same time she could not control.
She lost herself in the taste of his lips, in the
hard pressure of his body against her. . . .

MARY CARROLL
is an internationally known American writer
who has published here and abroad. She brings
to her romantic fiction a varied background of
teaching and traveling that gives her a unique
insight into the world of romance.

Dear Reader:

Silhouette Romances is an exciting new publishing venture. We will be presenting the very finest writers of contemporary romantic fiction as well as outstanding new talent in this field. It is our hope that our stories, our heroes and our heroines will give you, the reader, all you want from romantic fiction.

Also, *you* play an important part in our future plans for Silhouette Romances. We welcome any suggestions or comments on our books and I invite you to write to us at the address below.

So, enjoy this book and all the wonderful romances from Silhouette. They're for *you!*

P. J. Fennell
President and Publisher
Silhouette Books
P.O. Box 769
New York, N.Y. 10019

MARY CARROLL

Shadow and Sun

Silhouette Romance

Published by Silhouette Books New York

SILHOUETTE BOOKS, a Simon & Schuster Division of
GULF & WESTERN CORPORATION
1230 Avenue of the Americas, New York, N.Y. 10020

ISBN: 0-671-57002-1

First Silhouette printing May, 1980

10 9 8 7 6 5 4 3 2 1

Chapter 1

Britt Ryan lay back in the sweet smelling grass and gazed with a mixture of awe and irritation at the Chateau de Laon topping the crest of a nearby hill. Quartz-flecked, the great edifice cast a sentinel effect over the countryside, its sparkling battlements and turreted towers standing as stolidly inaccessible against the blue sky as a sugar castle in a fairy tale. The chief difference being, Britt thought, that the lord of the manor was an ogre and not a prince.

If Philippe Dolman were a man of his word, she might at this moment be snapping photographs behind those impressive stone walls, not sharing a meadow with three white cows two kilometers away. Her budget allowed for only one week in this Mediterranean area of France near the Spanish border, and three days of that were already gone.

Dolman, sunning himself in Majorca, would return when he chose and not a moment sooner, according to the gatekeeper who was not at all impressed that Monsieur Dolman had already missed by two days keeping his appointment with Sydney Fernham.

True, Britt Ryan was not Sydney Fernham, but the gatekeeper didn't have to know that. The given name was as proper a one for a girl as for a man, and until she was allowed to meet Philippe Dolman face to face, she had no intention of explaining why she was here representing herself as a male photographer of the Paris magazine *La Revue*, or how she happened to have in the pocket of her jacket his letter of introduction.

To say nothing of his camera, she thought with a wry smile. Poor Sydney. He would claw down every rope and pulley holding him in traction at Sisters of Mercy Hospital if he knew she'd taken not a single photograph for his deadline in a few weeks.

But what could she do?

Until Dolman returned, she couldn't set foot on the chateau grounds. The two Doberman pinschers leashed to the arm of the surly gateman had made that plain enough.

Sighing, she stood and dusted her tan riding pants. Too bad she didn't have a horse to go with them! Her daily treks on foot from the hotel in Perpignan through the autumn countryside were pleasant enough in the crisp morning air, but she was glad today she had thought to bring along a lunch of cheese and bread to break the return trip under a warmer sun. At least now in the early afternoon a few clouds were coming up.

Shading her eyes, she lifted them toward the sky— then caught her breath. What had momentarily blotted out the sun was not a cloud at all, but an enormous balloon, striped red and white and floating lightly as a butterfly directly toward her. Dangling beneath it in a golden gondola, a dark-haired man—one arm about the shoulders of a blond girl beside him—caught sight of Britt and leaned out, calling, "Bon jour, mademoiselle!"

Britt caught a glimpse of a wide, sensuous mouth turned up in a tantalizing grin, a strong chin set with a cleft, and searching eyes beneath dark brows. For an instant she could imagine herself extending her hand

and being drawn up beside him. Tingling excitement danced on her spine. How fabulous to drift through space in that exotic contraption—and with such a partner!

"Bon jour!" she called. But she was too late, she realized, for the intriguing balloonist to hear.

Quickly she snatched up the camera from the grass, and just as the balloon floated into line with two turrets of the chateau, she clicked the shutter.

"Oh, Sydney!" she breathed. "Just wait until you see that!"

"Perrier, please." Britt gave the waiter a smile and settled herself in a wire chair on the terrace of the hotel. Beyond her the River Tet twinkled with hundreds of tiny lights and the sweet smell of flowers sharpened by the twilight mingled with what she imagined was the salt air of the sea.

She said as much to the waiter when he returned, but before he could answer, a broad-shouldered man sitting at the next table turned to comment. "It *is* the sea you smell, though it's seven miles away. The wind is right this evening."

Britt stared in stunned delight. "Why, you're the balloon man!"

The tantalizing smile that had stirred her in the meadow appeared on his lips. "I recognized you at once when you crossed the terrace," he said.

And no wonder! Britt's hand flew to tuck in the black ringlets that had worked their way from beneath the beret she wore jauntily cocked over one eye. She was still attired in the same tan riding pants, rumpled plain shirt and worn suede jacket in which she had tramped across the countryside.

During the hours since her return she had been too busy exploring the shops and gardens of the quaint little town to bother changing her clothes, and when she decided to dine in a kitchen cafe she had discovered on a side street, there seemed no need to.

But here on the hotel terrace among other guests dressed for the evening, she must look like a tramp! A blush the shade of a wild rose flooded her creamy cheeks. But the balloonist, who without invitation had swung around to join her at her table, seemed intent only upon making himself comfortable.

"I've never seen anything quite so thrilling," she stammered, "as your balloon in that blue sky this afternoon."

His dark-eyed gaze shifted slowly to take in the high color of her cheeks. "Really? You're not accustomed to balloons?"

All at once she felt like a child. "I've seen a few, but not at such close range."

His glance moved from the hollow of her throat to the top button of her shirt. "I could have plucked off your beret."

"I know." Darn her heart for pounding so! He was rude, this arrogant stranger. In a moment she would say good night and leave him sitting alone.

He leaned back and regarded her coolly. "What were you doing out there? Having a picnic all by yourself?"

The sarcasm underlying his words ruffled her further. "Not exactly," she answered stiffly. "I'm here on assignment, but thanks to a rather thoughtless gentleman, I've been unable to get my work done."

"So you're lolling about the fields instead?"

"I was having lunch before walking back to town!"

"Ah, I see." He looked about restlessly. "Let's have some wine, shall we?"

"No, thank you."

But he was already motioning to the waiter. "Cotes-du-Rhone," he commanded. "And I drink it cold."

Britt rose. Frowning up at her he said, "You're not going?"

"I'm afraid I must."

"But I've ordered wine." He stood and reaching behind her, pulled her chair nearer to his. "Sit down. I want to hear more about this unreasonable oaf who's left you at loose ends in our charming countryside."

With a firm hand on her shoulder, he pressed her down into the chair. "You aren't French, are you?"

"I'm English," she replied, furious at herself for giving in to his insistence. "But I'm working in Paris."

The wine came. He tasted it and filled her glass. "What kind of work do you do?"

"I'm—a photographer."

"Oh." He grimaced. "One of those."

The nerve! She ought to slap his face, Britt thought. "You have something against photographers?"

He gave her a bored look. "Only one in particular who's made a nuisance of himself trying to interview me."

Who was this man sitting much too close? Britt thought in sudden panic. Someone she should know? A famous balloonist perhaps?

"I finally agreed to see him," the man went on. "But now I wish I hadn't."

Britt went on staring at him. If he'd had the courtesy to introduce himself, she might have recognized the name. "Perhaps the interview won't be too bad."

A slow smile erased his displeasure. "Perhaps he won't show up." He lifted his wine glass. She saw how even his white teeth were, the way his dark hair fell over his brow and curved onto his cheek in thick sideburns that lent a contoured look to his face and set off heavy brows above a straight, aristocratic nose.

How annoying that he made her feel like a knock-kneed schoolgirl when he was so attractive! Probably he amused himself in his spare time by bowling over lady tourists.

She drew herself up. "I'm Britt Ryan. I don't believe I caught your name."

He ignored the comment. "Ryan? You said you were English."

"My father was Irish."

"Then you ought to say so and not leave a fellow puzzling over where you got those remarkable green eyes." He gave her another disarming smile. "Though I should have guessed they came from the Emerald Isle."

"They came from Land's End," she replied curtly. "I was born there."

"Oh?" He twirled his wine glass lazily. "Let me guess. Your father was a herdsman."

"A seaman," she answered and could have bitten her tongue off. What business was it of his?

But he seemed genuinely interested. "Where did he sail from?"

"Mostly out of Plymouth. I lived with an aunt."

"Not your mother?" he said softly.

"My mother died when I was ten." Maybe he was a psychiatrist, she thought fleetingly. He was so skilled at drawing out information!

"I was fourteen when I lost mine." He scowled suddenly. "She ran away with an Italian count."

"Oh. I'm sorry."

He fixed a solemn stare on her. "You sound as though you mean it."

She blushed. "It couldn't have been pleasant for you."

"Oh, it wasn't so bad. I never cared for her actually."

"Never cared for your mother!" Britt's green eyes widened. "I never heard of such a thing."

He gave a little laugh. "Then that's two new experi-

ences you've had today. Almost having your hat lifted
by a passing balloonist, and sharing a drink with a man
who disliked his mother." He lifted his glass. "I think
you'll find when you grow up there are more of the
latter around than you ever imagined."

Britt pushed her chair back abruptly. "Thank you for
the wine."

His arm shot out to detain her. "You haven't even
tasted it."

"Then save it. Perhaps someone more mature will
come along whom you can force it on."

He grinned, and rising, caught her elbow. "I see I'm
guilty of a double sin." Her heart thudded crazily under
his dark-eyed scrutiny. "Underestimating your age and
forcing a drink on you. Will you forgive me?"

"Neither matters."

"Both do," he replied, and to her amazement she
found herself seated again. "I've been exposed to the
graces on one or two occasions," he said with a twinkle.
"Please give me a chance to prove it."

"I really must go."

"Why?"

She caught her breath. "And you claim to have
manners!"

He threw back his head and laughed. "You couldn't
have come from Land's End. You're prickly as a desert
cactus!"

"And you're the rudest man I've ever met!"

He sobered instantly. "I'll wager I am." His tanned
hand came out and covered hers on the table. Immediately she tried to withdraw it, but he held on firmly,
slipping his other palm beneath it. "Britt Ryan," he
said softly, "I think you've led a sheltered life."

Her face grew crimson. "I have not! I worked in a tea
shop from the time I was ten. I've known all types."

"And served them clotted cream?" He spoke in the same soft tone, never taking his eyes from hers.

"It wasn't that kind of tea shop. We sold it by bulk. And coffee too. I ran the grinder."

He put his head to one side. "Did you now?" A strong thumb massaged the bottom joint of her index finger. "I love the smell of fresh coffee."

"One grows tired of it," she replied before she could stop herself.

"You see," he said quietly, "what a civilized conversation we're having?"

She released an exasperated sigh. "*Why* are we having it?"

"Why?" He lifted his thick brows. "Because when I leaned from my gondola this afternoon and looked down at your pixie face in the meadow, I made up my mind I wanted to know you."

"I don't believe that." But it might be rather nice if she could!

He bit back a smile. "Then what's your explanation?"

"I think you were bored out here with no one to talk to. When you saw me crossing the terrace, you thought you'd have a little fun."

The smile played about his lips. "I am having fun."

"Which proves my point," she answered huffily.

"Do you think—" He turned her small hand over in his larger one and studied her palm. "That I couldn't find someone else with whom to amuse myself if I chose?"

She snatched her hand away and laid it quickly in her lap. "I haven't noticed anyone hovering about."

"Then take a look behind you." He leaned back to watch her head swing around.

Crossing toward them was a tall slender girl dressed

in a clinging white dress. Her silky blond hair brushed her shoulders, and she moved with the graceful ease of a jungle cat.

"Margo," the man said in response to Britt's puzzled look as she returned her gaze to him. "Don't you recognize her?"

"Why should I?"

"She was with me this afternoon."

In the gondola! With a shock Britt realized that though she had been aware of the presence of a woman, she'd had eyes only for the man.

The balloonist smiled knowingly. "She won't take it kindly that she failed to make an impression."

"Then don't tell her," snapped Britt.

The man rose as the beautifully dressed girl approached, and Britt wished with all her heart she could dissolve under the table.

"Margo St. Croix," he said smoothly, "meet the maid from the meadow." With an amused glance at Britt he pulled out a chair for the girl on his other side. "Her name is Britt Ryan."

Tawny eyes flecked with gold took Britt's measure. "You look as though you've just come in."

"From the meadow?" Britt's face went hot. "As a matter of fact, I have. I like to take my time when I walk." She pushed her chair back and stood. "I only stopped to refresh myself with a glass of Perrier before going up to my room." She forced a smile. "Nice meeting you. Have a pleasant evening."

"Do get some rest." The man's dark eyes twinkled. "After that strenuous journey, you must be exhausted."

Who *was* that rich boor who amused himself at the expense of others? Britt fumed—as she'd been doing for hours. Pity the poor photographer he'd maligned. And that girl! Ten to one she had retractable claws. What kind of copy would a couple of arrogant snobs like those two make? Who'd want to read it?

But still she couldn't get the balloonist out of her mind—and worse, she admitted finally, she didn't want to.

Retracing her steps to the window, she stood glaring defiantly down at the river lighted like a fairyland. But the scent of hothouse lilies of the valley floating from a bouquet on the dresser assailed her, and she collapsed suddenly on the window seat, dismayed at the ache within her.

What was she doing here alone in this hotel room with only a few francs left in her purse and her only hope for tomorrow a harebrained scheme that wasn't materializing? She didn't care about a career. All she truly wanted was someone to love and to love her, someone who'd wake up beside her in the morning and look at her as if she were the treasure of his life.

She wasn't a beauty, of course, like that willowy Margo. She was too short, too rosy-cheeked in times of crisis, too—how had he said it?—pixie-faced. But she had looks enough so no man need be ashamed of her. Unless she were wearing a dirty pair of riding breeches and a wrinkled shirt! The contrast between herself and Margo must have been shocking. No wonder the balloonist had thought her a joke.

A tremor rippled through her. Now *there* was a pair of eyes to wake up to. Liquid, glowing. And his hands. How strong and protective they were. How tenderly he had held hers. Her heart began a slow pounding. She leaned against the window ledge and closed her eyes.

Imagine floating over the countryside in the company of a man like that. Only he'd have to be gentle, not caustic as he'd been when he spoke of his mother. And he would have to be gallant, not rude. She could almost feel his lips against her ear, covering her mouth. Soft, warm persuasive lips . . . exploring lips . . .

The telephone jangled.

Britt shot up from the window seat. Sydney? But it was nearly midnight. Surely in a hospital—

It rang again. She crossed quickly and lifted the receiver.

"Britt?" The voice was crisp, authoritative.

"Who is this?"

"I can scale tall buildings in a single leap. I'm swifter than a zephyr—"

The balloonist! "Are you drunk?"

A hearty laugh came over the wire. "Of course I'm not drunk. Are you still awake?"

"You might have wondered that *before* you rang," she replied sharply.

The line exploded in a sigh. "You're the touchiest creature. Don't you ever laugh at anything?"

"I have a wonderful sense of humor!"

"I'm delighted to hear it."

"What do you want anyway?" she said crossly.

"I called to find out what you're doing tomorrow."

"What difference does it make?"

He sighed again. "Just answer my question."

"I wasn't aware you'd asked one."

There was too long a pause. Her pulse leaped. He hadn't hung up, had he?

"Miss Ryan."

She breathed a sigh of her own. "Yes?"

"Let's drive to Marseilles tomorrow."

"Marseilles! Are you insane?"

"My dear girl, people go there every day. They've even built roads for that purpose."

She laughed in spite of herself. Instantly he voiced his approval. "There! Doesn't that make you feel better?"

She ignored the jibe. "I can't go running all over the country. I'm a working girl."

"But you're not working now. You told me that yourself."

"I wasn't working today, but tomorrow I'd better be, or I'll have to wait on tables or something."

His voice sobered. "That bad? Anything I can do to help?"

He almost sounded as if he meant it. "Thanks," she said in a warmer tone, "but I'll manage somehow."

"Who is this rogue who keeps evading you? I'll go and punch him in the nose."

She laughed again. "He'd be certain then to welcome me with open arms, wouldn't he!"

"He'd better, or I'd know the reason why."

"I'd almost be willing to let you have at him, if I could only get hold of him."

"There, you see." His tone was low, persuasive. "He isn't available, so you can't work. There's no alternative but for you to go to Marseilles with me."

"In the balloon?" she said, only half teasing.

He laughed. "Don't I wish! But I'm afraid we hung her up on an apple tree after we left you."

"You didn't!"

"The nylon has a three-foot rip to prove it."

Britt saw again the dazzling splendor of the balloon as it passed over the valley. "But that's terrible!"

"Isn't it? The midday wind was too high. But never mind. In a few days I'll have her patched up. In the meantime, there's always the automobile. Mundane, but useful."

"I'm sorry I can't go with you." With a little shock she realized how much she meant it. "Early in the morning I have to strike out again and see if I can track down my man."

"What a terrible conscience you have. Why not be more like me? I have an appointment too, but I'd never let a little detail like that interfere with something I'd rather do."

"Bully for you." She hoped he caught her sarcasm. "Too bad we can't all be that carefree."

She heard his exasperated sigh. "Well, if you're absolutely set on going, I'll drive you."

"What? You'd be bored to death!"

"Try me and see." The warmth in his voice enabled her to see his eyes again.

"Well—"

"Judging from the time it took you today, it must be a terribly long walk." His tone grew teasing. "Ride with me; you may even make it back to the hotel before nightfall."

She gave up, laughing. "Oh, all right, if you insist."

"What time shall I pick you up?"

"How about nine?" A thought struck her. "I don't even know your name."

"Don't worry. I know yours. It's Irish. Your father was a seaman and a violator of child labor laws."

"Will you be serious!" Then a new thought popped into her mind. "Will your friend be coming too?"

She heard his low laugh. "Margo? Hardly. Anyway, she's in Nice by now, or at least I hope so. One crash per day is enough."

"Do you mean she flew there tonight?"

"That's where I've been. Seeing her to the airport. She took enough luggage for a month's stay. Listen, you'd better ring off and get some sleep, or you'll be all bleary-eyed for your ogre tomorrow." She heard him take a long, slow breath and let it go. "Pleasant dreams."

Replacing the receiver, she was aware that the husky voice persisted in her ear. What was it about him that was so compelling? she wondered. What caused her to feel weak simply thinking about driving through the countryside with him tomorrow? He was arrogant and caustic. Rude.

She took a breath to slow her pounding heart. But he was also charming, she admitted, and even a little sweet. Which was his true nature?

Perhaps he didn't have one. A warning note struck in her brain.

Chapter 2

"Will you please slow down!" With one hand Britt hung on to her beret and with the other, gripped the door of the smart little Ferrari.

White teeth gleamed in her companion's tanned face. "Am I frightening you?"

"You're scaring the stuffing out of me!" At the hotel the staccato beat of her heart had been easily attributable to the sight of the balloonist's lean, muscular form displayed to best advantage in tan chinos and an open-necked shirt and to the way his dark eyes carefully appraised her, but now it hammered from sheer terror that at any moment they would both be thrown out into the roadway.

She raised her voice over the roar of the motor. "There's not the least hurry, you know. He probably won't even be there, and even if he is, I can't very well talk to him if I'm lying in the ditch with a fractured skull!"

The man at the wheel laughed, but he took his foot off the accelerator and allowed the car to coast down into the misty valley. At the bottom he turned to her with a wide grin. "How's that?" he said.

She put her hand on her heart. "Better—though it may take me a while to recover."

"Then we'll rest." He whipped the automobile off into the shade of a small clump of lemon trees and stopped the motor.

Mixed feelings of annoyance and anticipation collided headlong in Britt's brain. "We haven't time to stop."

He lifted a dark eyebrow. "You've just assured me there's no hurry."

She colored. "But we don't have all *that* much time."

Watching her edge toward the door, he said, vastly amused, "I think you're more afraid of me than of my driving."

"I certainly am not!"

"Perhaps it's yourself you fear then."

"What a ridiculous idea." But she hoped her shirt collar hid the pulse going wild in her throat. He was quite possibly the most desirable man she'd ever met and quite the most cocksure as well. It would never do for him to know the unsettling effect his smoldering gaze had upon her. "It's just that you don't seem to realize how important it is for me to get there."

He shrugged, eyes glinting with mischief. "Get where? That's the only reason I've stopped. There's a fork in the road ahead. How can I know which direction to take unless you at least tell me where we're going?"

"The Chateau de Laon," she replied promptly.

The balloonist opened his mouth as if to speak, but no sound came.

"Do you know it?" said Britt.

"I've heard of it."

"But do you know how to get there?" she insisted. "I don't. Back down the road a way you turned left when I would have turned right, but you were going too fast for me to try to stop you. Now I'm completely lost."

Some of his color had come back. "I think I can find it."

"Fine, then." She folded her arms beneath her high young breasts. "Shall we go?"

But he had settled back into his seat, making no attempt to start the motor. "First I think you should explain what you want to do when you get there."

Britt frowned. "I've told you. Three days ago I had an appointment with Philippe Dolman to take some photographs of the chateau."

"You said you were on assignment and some fellow had been giving you the run-around. You didn't mention the chateau. You didn't mention Philippe Dolman."

Britt blinked. "Do you know him?"

A momentary flicker appeared in his dark eyes. "Why do you ask?"

"Something in the way you said his name."

"It's rather well-known," he answered brusquely.

Britt turned down the corners of her mouth. "And don't think he doesn't take advantage of that! The way he throws his weight around makes me sick."

He stiffened. "What do you mean?"

"It's perfectly obvious, isn't it? We peasants depend

upon people like him to make our living, and he doesn't even bother to show up for his appointments. He could care less what's happening to us."

"How do you know what's detained him?"

Her green eyes sparked fire. "Are you defending him?"

"Somebody should," he answered a bit lamely. "Anything could have happened to the poor fellow."

"I'll believe that when I hear it," she sniffed. "He's having too good a time in Majorca, that's all. And there's poor Sydney wired to his toenails at Sisters of Mercy, thinking all the while I have everything well in hand here."

"Sydney." Her companion said the name as if it were the missing piece of a jigsaw puzzle he'd just uncovered from beneath a corner of the carpet.

"Sydney Fernham." Britt had the grace to blush. "You see, it's something of a swindle actually. Sydney is the one who has the appointment, but he's broken both legs, and the copy for the article and the photographs have to be on the editor's desk the middle of next month."

"Wait." He fixed bright eyes upon her. "Start at the beginning. What happened to Sydney?"

"He had a skiing accident." She squirmed uncomfortably. "Well, not quite. He fell out of the chair lift on the way up the slope."

A reluctant smile curved the sensuous lips. "Go on."

"Look, we don't have all morning. It's already nine-thirty and—"

But he held her with his unrelenting gaze. "We have time for this."

"Well." She hesitated. "I suppose it's only fair to give you some kind of explanation since you've gone to all the trouble to drive me out here. I can at least fill you in on the main facts."

"An excellent idea," he murmured.

She sighed. "Here they are then. I work for a business service which supplies temporary secretarial assistance for Paris offices, and—"

"You said you were a photographer!"

"I am, but photography is only a hobby—so far. But if I can land this job—"

"Sydney's job?" he said in an acid tone.

She shot him a puzzled glance. "How can I explain if you keep interrupting?"

"A thousand pardons," he answered drily.

Her frown softened. If only his knee weren't touching hers, this would be all so much easier. "Sydney Fernham is on the staff at *La Revue*. He lives in the flat above me. Sometimes we have supper together."

"You see each other."

"No, we do not *see* each other!" she answered crossly. It was true that Sydney had lately made some rather pronounced romantic overtures, but the last thing she wanted was for this attractive man to think she was romantically involved with someone else. At least not until she was certain how she felt about him. "Sydney and I are friends."

He made no comment.

"He got me interested in taking pictures," she went on. "In the park, you know. By the river. That kind of thing. And I'm good at it. Really good!"

She moved away from him a bit and felt a stab of disappointment that he seemed not to notice. "I have an eye for composition, Sydney says, and he should know. He's tops. Then about two months ago—" She hesitated, possessed suddenly with the uncomfortable feeling that the man staring so fixedly was no longer interested in her, but only in what she was saying.

"Two months ago," he prompted.

"My office sent me to help out at *La Revue*, and that's when I discovered what a fabulous place it is."

"You decided you wanted to work there permanently."

She nodded. "But not as a flunky. On the staff, taking pictures. And if Philippe Dolman would only cooperate, I might have a chance."

"And if he doesn't cooperate?"

"I may murder him!"

A glint came into the dark eyes. "He might wish to do the same if he could hear you now."

Britt grinned impishly. "I wouldn't blame him actually. It's no good to be hoodwinked." Then her tone changed. "But he won't be sorry if he lets me have my way. I'll do a good job. Besides—" She lifted her chin saucily. "He owes it to the French people."

"What do you mean?" said her startled companion.

"Philippe Dolman owns the most gorgeous chateau in the whole of France and not half a dozen people out of his own tight little circle have ever even seen it."

A softer note came into his voice. "You consider it beautiful, do you?"

"I should say!" Her eyes grew starry. "The architecture, the paintings—"

"How do you know?"

"I saw it." She made a face. "Well, not really. Just half a dozen photographs. You see, one of my first tasks at *La Revue* was to research some back copies, and in one of them was an article about a diplomatic dinner held at the chateau—let's see. When was it?"

"April, a year ago."

Britt blinked.

"It was in all the papers," he said quickly.

"Was it? I didn't notice. I wasn't interested then."

"Why are you now?"

She frowned. "I've told you. Way back last spring Sydney got this assignment to do an in-depth feature of any chateau he chose." She shook her head despairingly. "And what did he pick? Chenonceaux. *Everyone* has seen Chenonceaux. No imagination whatsoever. What he needed was a spectacular subject."

The man across from her eyed her with reluctant admiration. "So after you saw the photographs of the Chateau de Laon, you gave it to him?"

She laughed gleefully. "I did! But he had a terrible time setting up the interview. Dolman was the most obstinate creature you can imagine."

A grim smile creased the tanned cheeks. "Maybe Monsieur Dolman enjoys his privacy."

"Oh, he definitely does. And he isn't entitled to it. Not so much of it anyway." She settled back down in the seat and said smugly, "If you want to know what I think, I think the Chateau de Laon ought to be taken away from him and given to the French government so all the people could enjoy it, not just one stuffed shirt."

"In much the same way some castles in your country belong to the National Trust?" he asked indifferently.

"Yes," Britt replied, "and those that are privately owned are shared with the general public. Visitors from all over the world come to admire and learn about their history." There was no response from the stern profile beside her, but she could not resist talking to such a captive audience about her favorite project. "If I can pull off this assignment, Sydney is going to do what he can to see that I'm taken on at *La Revue*." She warmed to her topic. "It's a very influential magazine, you know. I may just have to put a bug in his ear."

"Do you mean you'd try to stir up public opinion and force Dolman to give up the chateau?"

Her eyes sparkled. "Why not?"

He sat staring at her for a moment. Then abruptly he

turned the key and floorboarded the accelerator. Britt felt herself thrown back against the leather upholstery as the car shot out into the road. Fields and fences rushed past.

Britt was speechless. Then as they took a turn on two wheels, she shrieked, "What in the world is the matter with you? Do you want to kill us?"

"I want to be absolutely certain you keep your appointment," he shouted back.

"I hope to heaven I have a chance!" Three white chickens missed death by an inch and flew squawking into a meadow. "I'll tell you one thing, you madman," she screamed. "If you know what's good for you, you'll slow down before you get to the chateau or that gatekeeper will probably shoot you!"

A muscle rippled in his jaw. "Do you really think so?"

"Yes, I do! Watch out! We're coming to it." Her voice rose hysterically. "There's the gate!"

"And there's the gatekeeper."

Britt saw a man and two Doberman pinschers flash by in a blur orchestrated by the deafening blast of a horn. The gates slid open. The Ferrari sailed through.

"You murderer!" Britt raged as they came to a halt in a spray of gravel before the imposing chateau she was too stunned even to notice. "You could have killed us both!"

He shut off the motor and turned a contemptuous look on her. "We weren't for a moment in danger."

"Then you're blind—as well as stupid! We could have crashed right through the iron grillwork. I don't know why we didn't."

"We didn't because my horn activates the mechanism that opens it," he said coldly.

Britt's mouth fell open. "Why—you're—" She sucked in her breath. "You're Philippe Dolman!"

"How astute of you to guess." He opened the door on his side and got out. Over his shoulder he said, "If you're still interested in keeping your friend's appointment, I'd hurry if I were you. You're three days late already."

Chapter 3

"I think it was horrid of you not to tell me!"

Britt and Philippe Dolman were seated in a sunny garden room. Tea had been brought, and crisp pastry, but Britt had touched nothing. Acute embarrassment, anger and badly damaged pride had all but paralyzed her. To make matters worse, it was obvious that Philippe was enjoying her discomfort.

She glared across at him. How could she ever have thought that stony face attractive? And just last night she had called those obsidian eyes liquid and glowing. Philippe Dolman was a monster!

He spoke. "I suppose it hasn't occurred to you that it's I who should be offended?"

Did he think she was utterly stupid? Of course it had occurred to her! Why else would she be in such agony? She'd never get the interview and photographs now, and it was too late to make arrangements with another chateau. Sydney might even lose his job. "You brought it on yourself," she snapped.

He eyed her coldly. "That's to be your defense, is it?"

"It's the truth. You deliberately led me on just to hear what I'd say. It's not my fault your trick backfired."

He got up suddenly and set his cup on a marble tabletop. "You tricked *me.*"

"I didn't trick anyone!"

"No? Two days in a row you introduced yourself as Sydney Fernham to my gateman. That's not a trick? And you told me yourself your coming here was a swindle."

"*Something* of a swindle, I said. What you haven't given me the opportunity to explain is that the minute I came face to face with you, I intended to be frank about everything."

"Why should I believe anything you say? You lied once."

"Only to get past the gatekeeper!" If she could make him understand that much at least, then maybe something could be salvaged from the horrible mess she'd made of things. "Can you see that man out there paying the slightest attention to my story about Sydney falling out of the chair lift?"

Dolman's mouth twitched at one corner, but Britt saw only his stern frown and went on at a furious rate. "Once past him and those wretched dogs, I would have openly declared myself. I don't need to masquerade as Sydney. I have my own portfolio of significant work."

In a lofty tone he mimicked her words from the car. "Photographs of the park? The river? That sort of thing?"

Her green eyes iced over. "Among others. You

would have had complete assurance I could do competent work before I started."

He looked about innocently. "Where is it?"

"Where is what?"

"The portfolio."

She flushed. "At the hotel, of course. Surely not even you would expect me to burden myself with a briefcase while I walked from Perpignan."

"Today you rode."

Her color deepened. "I forgot it."

"You forgot it." He lifted skeptical eyebrows. "This was to be your big morning, I understood. Do-or-die day."

She jumped up, almost overturning the tea tray. "You don't want to listen to me! You don't care in the least about being fair."

"Fair!" The word seemed to sting him as nothing else had. "Give me one good reason why I should treat you fairly."

He advanced menacingly. She backed away, dismayed that as angry as she was, the scent of his skin, mingled with a crisp, woodsy fragrance of shaving lotion, still had the power to stir her.

He enumerated her sins on his fingertips. "You persuaded your friend Sydney to harass me until I finally set up an appointment with him. You came here under a false pretext. You labeled me an obstinate stuffed shirt who isn't entitled to his privacy *or* to the chateau which has been in his family for six centuries, and, if that isn't enough, if you had succeeded in your loathsome scheme you would have done all in your power to launch a vicious campaign in your magazine to discredit me. And you expect me to be fair!"

Britt fell back a pace, stunned by his vehemence and by her own culpability. "I wouldn't really have launched a campaign against you. Until the moment I said that, I'd never thought of such a thing."

"But you found it a delicious idea! It held enormous appeal for you."

"I was joking! Couldn't you see that? And you accused *me* of not having a sense of humor."

Her reference to the bantering tone of their conversation the evening before momentarily silenced them both.

Britt spoke first. "I wish we *had* gone to Marseilles," she said quietly. "I'd have learned your name. All this unpleasantness could have been avoided."

"And your little scheme would have succeeded," he said ironically.

She bridled. "How would it have succeeded? Would you have excused me from palming myself off as Sydney Fernham? If you'd have done that *after* Marseilles, why can't you do it now?"

"I know too much about you now."

His smugness infuriated her. "You don't know anything about me! You think I'm a liar and a cheat, and I'm neither."

"I think you've done a fairly good job of convincing me that you're both."

"You *want* to be convinced. You want Chateau de Laon all to yourself. You can't stand the thought of anyone out of your social stratum catching a glimpse of that magnificent carved stairway or the *Cordelova* on your walls."

She flung her arm out in a wide arc that took in the whole of the room. "All this fetching plasterwork, these ornamental cornices might be cheapened if some poor little girl from the provinces got a peek at them."

He was looking at her with a peculiar intensity. "How do you know about *Cordelova*?"

"Even at Land's End children are taught to read," she said haughtily.

"Children read fairy stories. They don't trouble themselves finding out how wallpaper is embossed to simulate leather."

"I didn't say I know how it's done," she shot back, but most of the fire had gone out of her, and she turned her back on him to gaze out on a garden ablaze with late autumn color. She wished at this moment she were back at Land's End, that she might hear the comforting sound of the coffee grinder instead of the cold voice of Philippe Dolman.

"Most of this conversation has centered on you," she heard him saying. "Suppose I tell you how it happens *I'm* here today."

"You came in a balloon," she answered dully, not bothering to turn around.

"Yes, I did!" She heard the sharpness of his tone and was aware that he had crossed to stand behind her. "At risk of life and limb, I might add."

"You could have caught a boat." She swung around to face him. "As you so glibly told me, 'people do that sort of thing every day.'"

Before the last word was out he had her by the shoulders, his voice cutting fiercely through her sarcasm. "I'm going to explain this, and damn it, you're going to listen!"

Her heart came up in her throat. She had never seen anyone quite so angry.

"A hot air balloon is not a plaything. It can't be bundled up like an extra pair of socks and crammed into a suitcase. And it can't be launched just any day some featherbrained adventurer decides to take a ride. There has to be a sustaining wind of a proper velocity."

With every word, his anger seemed to increase.

"Three days ago," he went on grimly, "neither condition prevailed. Nor the next day either." He narrowed his eyes threateningly. "Nor the next. But because I had made an appointment with some fool from Paris, and I don't take my obligations lightly, I decided to return whatever the risk."

She wanted to remind him he hadn't been at all concerned about keeping his appointment when he proposed going to Marseilles today, but she didn't dare.

"Margo and I are damned lucky we only snagged in an apple tree," he concluded. "We could have gone down in the sea."

His tirade, overly dramatized or not, had visibly shaken Britt, but she made an attempt at recovery. "And that would have been my fault, I suppose?"

He jerked her to him. "No," he answered in a tight voice. "It would have been *my* fault for placing unnecessary importance on a trivial scheme designed to make your fortune."

She twisted free of his grasp, her creamy cheeks afire.

"I'm sorry you and *Margo*," she spit out the name, "imperiled yourselves for my sake. I'm sorry you ripped your balloon and cut short your capers on Majorca. But I'm not in the least sorry the interview is off."

She crossed the room quickly and snatched her jacket from the chair. "I wouldn't spend the next three days in your company if they *gave* me *La Revue*."

But before she reached the door, he caught her arm and swung her about. "Wait just one minute."

"What for?" she taunted. "So you can further play on my sympathies?"

He ignored the slur. "We are now past the point of

discussing how and why either of us happens to be here. We are now going to sit down, if you can control your abominable temper—"

Her mouth flew open, but he left no entry for her objections. "—and talk about the feasibility of your project."

"There *is* no project!"

"There damned well better be," he answered and dragged her unceremoniously back to her chair.

When he'd made certain she would stay where he had placed her, he poured himself a fresh cup of tea and sat down opposite her. "Well. What do you propose to do?"

She stared, incredulous. "You don't honestly think there's the slightest possibility we could work together after all that's been said here this morning?"

A glimmer flickered in his dark eyes. "We've cleared the air at least."

"Are you saying you want to be interviewed, that you want me to photograph the chateau?"

He set down his cup. "I'm saying I intend to fulfill the agreement I made with Sydney Fernham, and I expect you, as his surrogate, to go through with his end of the bargain."

Britt was stunned into silence.

Finally she said, "I'm not sure I have time now to do it properly."

"You have until the middle of next month, you said."

She surveyed him coldly. "You can't get through your head, can you, that I have to make a living? I could afford to spend a week here, no more, and half of that's gone."

"My fault." He spoke crisply. "I'll reimburse you for any expenses you will have after the time you originally set aside."

Britt blinked.

"Furthermore," he went on in a brisk tone, "I expect both the article and the photographs to be superior, so you will please take as much time as necessary to see that the highest standards of excellence are met."

All was not lost for Sydney after all! Maybe not even for herself if she handled with kid gloves this mercurial man who quite obviously believed himself to be a god. "I can guarantee quality," she said numbly.

"Good. That much is settled then. Will you start this morning?"

"I— Yes." Was this really happening? Five minutes ago he seemed on the verge of choking her, and now he was commanding her to begin work. "But I refuse to take any photographs until I've explored the place thoroughly," she added in an attempt to restore some part of her eroding authority.

"Very well." He got up. "I'll see that the staff is informed."

"You're being very decent about this," she began hesitantly.

His gaze settled on her, and she was aware once again of the devastating effect his concentrated attention had upon her.

She wet her lips. "I hope you'll forgive my— rudeness."

For a moment she was afraid he might counter her apology with sarcasm, but his penetrating gaze faltered, and he said quietly, "I was discourteous to you as well. Shall we forget it?"

"Yes! I'd like that very much."

She waited, believing in a moment his tantalizing smile would reappear and they would once again be on the same footing as when the morning had begun.

But instead, he walked away toward a desk in the

corner and began to flip through an accumulation of mail. When he became aware that she was still standing there, he turned and said with cold formality, "Was there something else?"

She felt her face go hot. "I— No. Except that I was wondering if there might be a particular part of the chateau you'd prefer I saw first."

A look of annoyance crossed his face. "It's your project. Suit yourself." And he returned his attention to his mail.

Chapter 4

The rest of the morning Britt wandered aimlessly through the long corridors of the chateau, scarcely noticing as she poked her head into one palatial apartment after another the grandeur that surrounded her.

All she could think of was the total disinterest with which Philippe Dolman had dismissed her. She might have been a speck of dust! Was that why he was allowing her to go ahead with her plans? So that at every turn he could humiliate her? Was ignoring her to be his way of getting back at her for that silly speech she'd made in the car?

She sat down on a brocade love seat at the head of the oak staircase and stared disconsolately at the intricate carvings which decorated it. He needn't bother to humiliate her. She'd done that herself. What a pompous little fool she must have appeared, ranting about how she would like to take away his chateau and give it to the French government, calling him a stuffed shirt and declaring herself to be as fine a photographer as Sydney.

She cast a dejected glance at the camera in her lap. An artist was the master of his craft's tools, and all she knew how to do was put the film in and click the shutter. If Sydney hadn't discovered her naturally keen eye for composition, she wouldn't be in this mess now.

Or if those first few photographs she'd shot at the Tuileries hadn't turned out so beautifully, she'd never have dreamed up this crazy scheme in the first place. Even if she had, Sydney would have laughed at her.

Her gaze moved up to an imposing portrait of a marquis on the opposite wall, and she thought dismally, *I don't deserve to be here. I ought to be typing letters in some dark cubbyhole on the Rue D'etretat. How I wish I were!*

A shuddering sigh escaped her.

"Tired already?"

Startled, she swung about to find Philippe Dolman studying her from the open doorway of the second floor library. His unexpected appearance sent a swift shock of admiration coursing through her. His strongly muscled frame was clothed in closefitting riding pants and his knit shirt opened at the throat to reveal a thick mat of the same dark hair which capped his head.

"I'm a little tired," she confessed weakly. "But mostly I'm overwhelmed." She hoped he couldn't guess by what!

He came toward her easily, and a surge of excitement

seized her. *He* certainly belonged here. In another age he might have been a king.

"Everything is even more wonderful than I imagined," she heard herself gushing, and despised the nervousness which inspired it. No man had ever had such a disquieting effect on her.

From beneath a furrowed brow he surveyed her. "Have you decided what to photograph first?"

Her thoughts scrambled about like startled mice. Snatching at one, she blurted, "The tower dungeon."

"What?"

She started up. "But if that displeases you, I can easily switch to something else."

His frown deepened. "Not at all. I think it's a first-rate idea. After all, if it hadn't been for the dungeon keeping 'safe' our enemies, there'd probably be no chateau at all." He put his head to one side and gave her a penetrating stare. "Perhaps that was your idea?"

It *had* been, when she'd first seen the dungeon, but she wasn't about to risk antagonizing him again. "Such a thought never occurred to me."

She saw at once her answer had annoyed him anyway. She quailed. The last thing she wanted was another scene.

But when he spoke, his voice held no anger, only resignation. "When we first met on the hotel terrace, you impressed me as a saucy, fiery little Irish girl who didn't give two pins for anyone's opinion."

Her heart sank. Saucy, he had said. Fiery.

"You verified that opinion when we spoke on the telephone and in the car this morning—and even for a while in the garden room."

His eyes bored into hers.

"But then you began displaying another side of

yourself—as you're doing now." His look pinned her like an insect to the love seat. "An obsequious side, a side in which humility almost borders on fawning." He stared coldly. "It's a side I'd rather not have seen."

Abruptly he turned and went toward the staircase. As he descended, he called back carelessly, "Luncheon is served in half an hour on the back terrace. You're expected."

When Britt had partially recovered from the stinging reproach Philippe Dolman had delivered with such nonchalance, she could scarcely contain her fury.

"Why that arrogant, aristocratic snob!" she stormed, pacing the wide hallway and brandishing her camera as if it were a sword. "The nerve of him, calling me obsequious!" That meant degradingly submissive, didn't it? Submissive—in a pig's eye!

She banged the camera into the palm of her other hand, but the blow served only to further incense her. Who did he think he was, she raged, that he could brazenly stomp on her sensibilities as if she were mere dirt beneath his Gucci boots!

Well, he'd asked for it, and he was certainly going to get it. She'd show him just how obnoxious she could be. Before she was through, he'd *beg* her to be humble! He hadn't the manners of a stable boy—nor the common sense either—or he'd have recognized the difference between sincere regret and fawning. He'd know the strength of character required to admit one's own error in front of an enemy. He was a clod! A nincompoop.

But gradually rage subsided into the simple ache of badly wounded feelings, and once more she sank onto the love seat, this time perilously close to tears. His treatment of her wouldn't matter half so much if she hadn't been so attracted to him or her imagination so

drawn to the sight of him in that dratted balloon . . .
She pressed her fingers tightly against her eyelids.
Wasn't it just like her to fall in love with a brute?

She sat up straight. Fall in love! The stone walls of
the chateau seemed to waver like a mirage. She
couldn't be in love. She hated the man!

Oh, did she? another part of her taunted. Why, then,
was she so upset? Ordinarily, as Philippe had guessed,
she cared little what other people thought of her, and
yet this man's opinion had wounded her to the quick.

Her throat closed around a sob. What was she to do?
Run as fast as she could? Take the first train back to
Paris? What about Sydney? He was counting on her.
What about her hopes for a job at *La Revue?*

The devil could take the job! she thought angrily.
She didn't want it anyway. She wanted a husband. She
wanted a home and children. But short of resigning
herself to Sydney, whom she thought of as a somewhat
bumbling younger brother, or placing an ad in "Situa-
tions Wanted," it looked as if she'd have to spend the
rest of her life alone. Philippe Dolman wasn't falling in
love with *her,* that was plain enough! Worse, she
obviously repulsed him now, and in the face of that,
how could she stay on here feeling as she did?

But how *did* she feel? she argued miserably. A part
of her loathed him, or at least loathed his insensitivity.
A part of her hated his brashness and arrogance.

Yet . . . whenever she remembered the way he had
held her hand on the hotel terrace . . . the way her skin
burned at the pressure of his knee. . . .

Something inside her gave way, as it did each time his
cool-eyed gaze touched any part of her. She couldn't
handle this! Not only was he physically magnetic, she
admitted hopelessly, but his whole personality drew her
to him. Every fiber of her being urged her to make

herself important to this man, to make herself so vital and indispensable that even in the briefest separation he would feel as if breath itself were taken from him.

But this was madness! Sheer nonsense. The romantic setting of the chateau was inspiring such fantasies. She'd known Philippe Dolman less than twenty-four hours. She'd never believed in love at first sight.

But neither had she ever felt as she did now. Be it love, simple physical attraction or a combination of the two, it had aroused feelings she'd never known could exist. With a sinking heart she realized as vulnerable as she felt now she'd never be able to withstand another attack of the sort Philippe had just delivered. The sensible course was to put as much distance between him and herself as she could.

But even as the thought formed, she recognized sadly that she had no intention of acting upon it.

How then was she to survive?

She sat on for a time, dully regarding the mosaic pattern of the tile beneath her feet. She was hopelessly trapped.

But slowly it came to her that Philippe himself had provided the key for survival. Coolness, aloofness. Her flagging spirits lifted with the glimmer of hope the thought provided.

If she could maintain the strictest privacy in the chamber of her heart— If she could manage not to give herself away by look or deed or word, then perhaps she had a chance to leave here with some portion of her pride intact.

After all, how long could this assignment last? Another week? Ten days at the most. In the presence of Philippe Dolman she would appear the model of efficiency and decorum—the same attitude she presented in the Paris offices where she went to type letters and take dictation. If Philippe were as middle-aged and paunchy as her usual employer she'd have no trouble, would she? Anyone could pretend for a fortnight!

Besides, she'd have periods of respite at the end of each day. She could return to the hotel in Perpignan and fall apart there if necessary without anyone being the wiser.

She stood up. A renewed confidence took hold of her. She could manage it!

Thank heavens for this luncheon too, she thought, hurrying down the stairs. It would provide just the opportunity she needed to impress Philippe with her new image before the old one imprinted itself indelibly on his mind. Pinning a tight little smile on her lips, she took a deep breath and opened the terrace door, feeling almost eager for the challenge.

A fresh breeze had sprung up from the west, and autumn sunlight filled the valley. To her right under a gay parasol she could see a table laid for the meal, and far away to her left through a golden haze, a rider on horseback taking a low fence with practiced ease.

Crossing to the edge of the terrace, she shaded her eyes with one hand. It shouldn't be—but it was. Philippe. She swung around and discovered the table was set only for one.

Her brave new resolves wilted. So he wasn't dining with her after all. She should have known the lord of the manor wouldn't sit down with the help.

Too bad such niceties hadn't mattered on the hotel terrace, she thought bitterly, taking her place at the table. He could have saved them both a lot of trouble. But he was slumming then, she supposed. A lump came up in her throat. And anyway, he hadn't known then what he knew now about her, as he had so plainly pointed out.

Her gaze went back to the valley. Horse and rider

were preparing to take the fence again. Automatically her hand went out and brought the camera to her eye. Remembering how she had swung it about in the upper hall, she wondered vaguely if it would operate at all. It might be a blessing if it wouldn't. She'd have no recourse then, but to return to Paris and forget she'd ever heard of the Chateau de Laon or its intriguing owner.

But the reassuring click came.

With a sigh she set the camera aside and cupping her chin in her hands, watched wistfully as Philippe Dolman atop his mount cleared the fence and cantered away.

Chapter 5

A Louis XII clock was striking five when Britt descended into the wide entry hall. The major part of the afternoon she had spent in the upper regions of the chateau, photographing first the dungeon tower and then a series of small apartments replete with hidden staircases, trapdoors and odd little nooks in which she decided political prisoners must at one time have taken refuge.

She was exhausted, but her sparkling eyes and rosy

cheeks belied her weariness. Her activities had transported her into another period of history, and when she saw Philippe Dolman standing, hands on his narrow hips, watching her descend the stairs, she realized with a start she hadn't given him a thought in hours. Perhaps working here at the chateau would not be such an impossible task after all.

"Finished for the day?" A leather riding jacket of burnt orange covered his open-necked shirt now and by his flushed face and the sharp scent of the outdoors which assailed her nostrils as she approached him, she concluded that he too had spent an exhilarating afternoon.

"I think I got some excellent shots," she answered.

"Of the tower?"

"And of the apartments adjoining it." Abiding by her noontime resolutions would be much easier, she thought with dismay, if he were not looking at her with such frank approval. Evidently Philippe Dolman's moods changed with the hour. "The apartments are cunningly designed."

He nodded. "Men of the cloth hid in them during times of persecution, I'm told. And at other periods, political dignitaries used them for hideouts whenever they needed to beat a quick retreat."

"I thought so!"

With a glance he took in her high color and sparkling eyes. "Come into the study. We'll have a sherry, and you can tell me what else you've discovered."

She was on the point of refusing, but he moved briskly ahead, leaving her no alternative but to follow. Swinging open a door, he led her into a cozy paneled room where a small fire burned in the grate. A decanter of wine and two glasses stood on a low table before it.

Her heart knocked. Had he been waiting for her?

"Sit down." He motioned toward the chair nearest the fire and took up the wine. For a moment a smile played on his lips. "I'm not forcing this on you, am I?"

It seemed a hundred years ago that she had accused him of that instead of just last night! "I'll enjoy it, thank you."

How difficult it was not to respond to his good humor with a smile of her own, but if she let down her guard, even for a moment, who knew what might happen?

He handed her the brimming glass. "Perhaps this will perk up your appetite. Cook tells me you only nibbled at your lunch."

Her face went hot, but he spared her the embarrassment of an answer. "I'm probably to blame. I came down rather hard on you, I'm afraid."

Quick tears stung behind her eyelids. Anger, she found, was a far easier emotion to bear than pity.

"I'm rather inept at dealing with the feminine mind," he went on in a softened tone. "I sometimes have difficulty remembering how sensitive a woman can be."

"It doesn't matter," she said quickly and took a sip of the wine. When she could trust her voice again she said, "Did you enjoy your ride?"

He appeared mildly surprised.

"I saw you from the terrace." She returned his look squarely. "In fact, I snapped your picture. *La Revue*'s readers are sure to want to see the owner of the chateau taking his leisure."

He chuckled. "Developing my equestrian skills is something more than a leisure time activity I'm afraid. Through the years the Chateau de Laon has been noted for its horses and its riders, and I'm bound to hold up the tradition though I much prefer taking to the air in a balloon than from the back of a horse."

"You compete then?"

He nodded. "But only in the meet held in autumn in Limoges. We always go up for that because in conjunction with it we can spend some time at my farm which is nearby. I have twelve acres of walnuts dropping from the trees in this season."

We, he had said. Who did that mean? Margo? "I've never been to Limoges."

"The city is lovely, but it's the countryside that appeals most to me." He stretched his long legs toward the fire and sighed contentedly. "I love the crisp autumn mornings, heat in midday, and then the cooling off at night that demands a fire." He stared in silence at the flames.

In a moment he spoke again. "The fall rains begin about the same time as the meet, however, and generally we end up rushing out between showers, grabbing a hatful of nuts and rushing in again."

Britt blinked. "You pick them up yourself?"

He laughed. "Of course. It's fun."

"I'm sure it is." Her face colored. "I only thought—"

His disquieting gaze settled on her. "What did you think?"

"I hadn't imagined you'd consider nut gathering worthy of your time."

"It might be interesting to know what else you imagine about me," he replied coldly.

She set down her glass and got up. "One thing I imagine is that you have far more important things to do than to sit here chatting with me."

"If I did—" His tone was even. "I'd be doing them."

Their glances locked, and Britt felt an icy finger of excitement against her spine.

"I invited you in for a drink because I want to know you better. But that won't be possible unless you sit down again and make yourself comfortable until dinnertime."

"It's getting late," she heard herself say, though a part of her longingly pictured the two of them cozily ensconced before the fire while darkness gathered. "I've quite a long walk ahead of me."

He laughed. "What an absurd thing to say."

Her nostrils flared. "I don't see why."

"Because you're not going anywhere for one thing. And even if you were, I certainly wouldn't allow you to strike out alone this late in the day."

She felt a smothering sensation in her chest. "What do you mean, I'm 'not going anywhere'?"

"Just that. I had my man Rene go over to Perpignan with one of the maids and gather up your things at the hotel."

Her lips parted, but he went on before she could speak. "You said you were pressed for time. I thought I'd save you some."

She had all she could do to control her anger. The gall of the man, sending a couple of strangers to pack up her things!

"Well," she said, "if I'm no longer staying at the hotel, where *am* I staying?"

"In Margo's apartment for the next few days," he answered casually. "It's just beyond the library on the second floor. There are rooms I much prefer, but they're in the south wing." His eyes moved over her. "I thought you might be too lonely all by yourself out there."

Britt flushed. Obviously Margo was his mistress. But if he had any thoughts about Britt Ryan filling in for her on a temporary basis—or any other basis, for that matter—he had another think coming! "I doubt if Margo would appreciate my intrusion," she said coldly.

"Margo won't know. She'll be away for at least a week, and by that time the housekeeper assures me some redecorating I'm having done will be finished, and you can move into one of those rooms."

Britt drew herself up. "In a week I'll be gone."

He eyed her lazily. "I doubt that. We agreed, don't forget, that whatever you submit to your magazine has to be top-notch."

"I never intended otherwise," she said haughtily. "I want that job, remember?"

His jaw tightened. "You made that rather plain on the drive out this morning."

She felt her color rising. "I don't think it's at all necessary for me to stay here."

"Do you *mind* staying here?"

"I see no reason to."

"Then I'll give you one." He poured himself another glass of sherry and stood looking at her as if she were a schoolchild in need of stern discipline. "I have an erratic schedule. I never know from one hour to the next where I'll be."

"I'm quite aware of that," she answered drily.

"Then you won't find it difficult to understand that we'll have to work together at my convenience. When I have time for your questions, that's when I'll answer them."

What stunning arrogance! "Maybe I won't have any questions."

He smiled tolerantly. "That's hardly likely, is it?" Then he went on in the same authoritative tone with which he had begun. "I'm busy most days. Probably the only time I'll have free for you will be the evening. I'll want you here, not down the road in Perpignan."

She flushed. Certainly one could read more than one meaning into that!

"And another thing," he went on. "I'll want to go over your work very carefully. I shall be interested in the most minute details you submit to your magazine."

This last drew her up short. "You intend to censor what I write?"

"That's rather a harsh way of describing supervision, isn't it?"

"That depends upon what you mean by supervision."

He set down his glass with a sigh. "You enjoy being difficult, don't you?"

Britt's Irish temper flared. "Really, Monsieur Dolman! There's no pleasing you, is there? One moment I'm fawning and obsequious; the next, I'm difficult!"

He shot her a cool glance. "Perhaps soon you'll be able to strike a happy medium."

I'd much rather strike you! she thought angrily, but managed to control herself enough to say, "I'm sure if we tried, we could work out a time agreeable to us both, and one that would still allow me to go on staying at the hotel."

He gave an exasperated sigh. "What is it about the hotel that you find so attractive? This is the Chateau de Laon." His waving arm encompassed the room. "France's most beautiful, according to you. You have an opportunity to stay in it, Miss Ryan. Why don't you want to?"

"Because," came her haughty reply, "your living arrangements don't fit my style!"

For a moment he appeared stunned. Then a slow smile curved his sensuous lips. "Ah. I see."

"Fine! Then I'll gather my things and head back to Perpignan."

He advanced, dark eyes blazing. "Perhaps you are afraid I'll compromise you if you stay a moment longer under my roof?"

What a devil he was! "There's not the slightest chance of that," she snapped.

"No?" He stood so near she caught the male scent of

him and felt her knees go weak. "Then perhaps it's this you're afraid of."

Before she knew what was happening, he had his arms about her. His head came down. His mouth found hers.

She struggled fiercely, but only for a moment. The searching warmth of his lips, the insistent manner in which his embrace molded her to him set fire to her passions. Independent of logic or prudence, her need for him betrayed her, and she discovered herself returning his kiss, clinging to him with an ardor that appalled her, but which at the same time she hadn't the least inclination to control. The room receded. She lost herself in the taste of his lips, in the hard pressure of his body against her.

Finally they drew apart, staring at one another numbly.

Britt was the first to find her voice, though it came out only a whisper. "That wasn't very professional of me."

He pulled her to him, his strong hand firm at the nape of her neck. "Nor very bright of me," he said thickly. His hot breath curled in her ear, and longing raced again within her.

"You'll probably run like hell now," he murmured hoarsely. His lips moved to her temple, then back to her expectant mouth. "Probably we should both run— but in opposite directions."

The phone jangled loudly on the desk. They sprang apart. It rang again, and Philippe crossed swiftly to answer it.

Britt, still under the spell of his kiss, watched his dark brows come together in a sudden frown, heard his voice sharp with annoyance.

"Margo? Where are you?"

Britt's heart turned over.

Philippe's frown deepened. "But I wasn't expecting you before the middle of next week."

Dazed, Britt put together the rest of the conversation. Margo was coming back to the chateau though Philippe objected. Her arrival, he told her irritably, would interfere with a project he'd just begun.

Me, thought Britt with sickening insight. I'm the project, and naturally it would never do for his mistress to appear just as he was getting it underway! She felt her face catch fire. All she wanted now was to escape . . . to run like hell, as Philippe had said. Oh, if only she had!

She heard him hang up and turned to face him with a nonchalance she was far from feeling. "Is Margo returning?"

He nodded. "Though I don't know why." He was lost in thought for a moment. Then he said vaguely, "You'd better move your things."

It wasn't my idea to put them in her apartment, Britt felt like screaming. Instead she heard herself say mildly, "I hope my room is still available at the hotel."

He gave her an absent-minded look. "I'm sure it is, but we've already settled that question. You're staying here. You can choose whichever apartment in the south wing pleases you."

How handy! she thought bitterly. *Stashed away there, I'll be far enough removed from Margo so that if you're clever enough you can keep both pots boiling at once. It might be worth staying around just to watch you try!*

"I'll make the change after dinner," she said curtly.

"I think you'd better take care of it at once," he replied. "Margo was calling from Perpignan. She's on her way."

Chapter 6

In little more than a quarter of an hour Britt had transferred her meager possessions from Margo's suite of rooms to an elaborate apartment in the isolated south wing and was back again in the study, sitting stiffly in front of the fire with Philippe, awaiting the arrival of Margo.

Philippe glanced at his watch for the third time in as many minutes. "She ought to be here by now."

A cold knot settled in the pit of Britt's stomach. Since Margo's call, he had indicated in no way that he even remembered what the ring of the telephone had interrupted. She cast a sidelong glance at his chiseled profile, recreating in her mind a picture of the two of them in each other's arms. How tender he had been, how right she had felt enclosed in his embrace. And how suddenly it had all ended.

She swallowed. "Does Margo have her own car?"

"What?" Philippe stared at her as if for a moment he had forgotten she was there. "A car? No, not in Perpignan. Velosue, a local taximan, is driving her."

"She'll be along soon then," said Britt, wishing her words could magically produce the opposite effect and spirit Margo back to Nice.

Uneasily she remembered the catlike grace of the blonde, the tawny slanting eyes which had surveyed her coldly on the hotel terrace. There was sure to be a dreadful scene when she discovered the "maid from the meadow" had somehow, in a day's time, entrenched herself in the chateau, and Britt had had enough of scenes for one day.

Was it only this morning, she wondered dizzily, that Philippe had roared with blaring horn through the gates of the chateau, revealing himself as its owner? In the scope of a single day he had wounded her to the quick and sent her passions soaring to the sky.

His voice broke through the silence. "You're certainly solemn."

Why wouldn't I be? she longed to fling back. *I've fallen in love with you, and since Margo's call, you're hardly aware I exist.* Instead she said quietly, "I'm tired. It's been a long day."

"And it isn't over yet."

The bleakness in his tone stirred her numbed hopes. Was it possible he was no more eager for this encounter than she? Possible that what appeared to be impatience to see his mistress was actually dread?

"I've an idea," she said, starting up. "I'm really not hungry. What if I skip dinner and go on up to bed before Margo arrives? That would leave you free to explain in your own time what I'm doing here." She waited a moment. "Wouldn't that be better?"

He hesitated only an instant. "Perhaps it might."

It was the right answer and one she expected, but at the same time she felt as if a door had been shut in her face. "I'll hurry on then."

"Britt—" He got up and came toward her. "It must appear to you that I'm not handling this well."

A coldness squeezed her heart. "You needn't explain. I understand everything."

"How can you when I don't?" He laid his hand on her arm, and she felt an electric thrill sweep through her. "I ought never to have allowed what happened a while ago without first making clear what Margo means to me."

But Britt was sure she already knew what Margo meant to him. "It was only a kiss!" she said harshly. "It's already forgotten."

The effect of her words changed his expression like a whiplash. The softness around his mouth disappeared, and a hard glint came into his eyes. "I see. My mistake."

The coldness of his tone broke through her anger. She was on the point of retracting her words, but suddenly the furnishings of the room sprang out of the shadows. The door from the hallway swung open and light flooded the room. Margo, a willowy column in softest blue cashmere, stood on the other side.

"Well, hello!" Her tawny eyes swept the two of them still standing together. "Am I interrupting something?"

"Certainly not," said Philippe smoothly, moving toward her as she lifted her face for a kiss. "We were just about to give up on you and go in to dinner. What kept you?"

Margo's eyes lingered on his lips. "Velosue's rickety taxi. What else?"

Britt flushed, feeling as if she were part of an audience in a darkened theater waiting for the lovers on the stage to embrace.

But all at once Margo turned to her with a dazzling smile. "Whom have we here, darling?"

"Why, Britt Ryan," said Philippe. "I introduced you last night. On the hotel terrace."

Britt flinched. He might as well have said, she's the girl I picked up, remember?

"Oh, of course." Margo put out a slender hand and smiled. "How are you?"

Then, brushing past, she flung her leather gloves onto the sofa. "I hope Philippe has been showing you the chateau. He's much too selfish with it, you know." Looking from one to the other of them, she seemed completely at ease, not at all the angry feline Britt had expected.

Margo smiled bewitchingly. "The chateau is a treasure house of wonderful things, but Philippe is such an old hermit he likes to keep them all for himself."

Philippe frowned. "You know that's not true."

Margo laughed and turned conspiratorially to Britt. "He despises being told that, so I tell him as often as I can, just to rile him."

Britt managed a weak smile. Margo's words had almost echoed her own smug statement in the car, and she wondered if it were her conscience or Philippe's eyes—which she dared not meet—that seemed to be boring into her.

"Shall we go into dinner?" he said gruffly.

Margo hooked her arm in his and planted a kiss on his cheek. "Oh dear, now I've gone too far, haven't I? Shame on me." She halted and swung back toward Britt.

"But look at us, Philippe. Rushing in ahead of our guest as if she didn't exist." She linked her other arm in Britt's. "Do forgive us. When we're apart, even for a day, it seems like centuries, and once we're together again, I'm afraid we're not aware of anyone except each other."

"I can see that," said Britt stiffly.

"It's so unusual for us to have company," Margo chattered gaily. "Especially female company." She smiled up at Philippe. "It's quite delightful, isn't it, darling?"

Philippe's answer was an unintelligible mumble, and he passed ahead of them into the dining room, pulling out Margo's chair first, then Britt's.

She felt the pressure of his fingertips on her arms as he slid the chair beneath her and despised her faithless heart for pounding so. If, as she had suggested, she had gone up to bed without dinner, would Philippe have thought to remove this third place from the table? And if he hadn't, how would he have explained it to Margo?

Then, listening as he glibly launched into the story of Sydney Fernham and the chair lift, Britt acknowledged bitterly to herself that he would have had no more trouble explaining the extra place than he had had convincing her with only one kiss that he cared for her and no one else.

In her bedroom at last, Britt reflected that the meal she had just endured and the quarter hour's conversation afterward in the study was the longest, most painful ordeal of her life. Not even the endless weeks during which, as a child, she had waited out her father's voyages, had seemed so torturous.

But at least now, she thought, settling between the smooth linen sheets, she had been through the fire. The rest of the week while she finished the assignment should be child's play compared to it. Margo would occupy Philippe, and she could get on with her work, needing only to recall what she had learned at the dinner table in order to banish any wayward longings.

Margo and Philippe were engaged to be married.

She had heard the announcement from Margo's own

lips, and not a word of denial had come from Philippe. True, he had not exhibited a great deal of enthusiasm, but doubtless, Britt thought, her own prejudice had colored her appraisal.

The engagement would be announced publicly the weekend after the equestrian meet at Limoges, and it would be announced in grand style at a costume ball patterned after the account of another held in the chateau during an earlier century.

Margo had uncovered the old manuscript herself in which the details were given, and for months she had been at work consulting with costumers in Paris, artists from the Barbizon area, and musicians from St. Tropez.

Margo had embarked then on the guest list which, it seemed to Britt, would include half the titles of Europe. While his fiancée had elaborated, Philippe had said little, occupying himself with his food and glancing only occasionally from Margo's animated face to Britt's frozen one, fixed in a polite little smile.

She was lucky she supposed, tossing about in the canopied bed, not to have made a bigger fool of herself than she had already done. What if Margo hadn't come back tonight?

Immediately a parade of fantasies began behind her eyelids: Philippe embracing her in the tower, pulling her up behind him on his horse, leaning from the staircase to kiss her.

Stop it! she commanded herself and sat up in bed, grateful for the moonlight which illuminated every feature of the elegant room and brought reality sharply into focus.

She must concentrate on what truth she could find in this situation, not on how badly it hurt.

Philippe, not unlike most of his countrymen—and

men the world over, she supposed—responded positively to an attractive female; and obviously he had found her attractive to some extent or he would not have bothered to phone her in the middle of the night and invite her to drive to Marseilles.

But that action and the resultant scene in the study this afternoon were separate and apart from the mainstream of his life: his plans with Margo.

I was to be only an interim distraction, she thought, swallowing back her tears. Plainly Philippe had decided during Margo's absence to entertain himself with the naive little innocent he'd caught sight of leaning from his balloon and had wasted no time in moving her from her hotel into his lair.

But there her sense of fairness halted her musings. When they had started out this morning for the chateau, Philippe had not even known where they were headed. It was Sydney Fernham he planned eventually to meet at the chateau, not Britt Ryan.

But—she quickly countered—it must have occurred to him while they were quarreling in the morning room that Lady Luck had played directly into his hands; thus his insistence that Britt stay and fulfill Sydney's commitment. He'd have his little fling, and then by the time Margo returned Britt would be gone, and no one would be the wiser except the servants.

Probably everything would have gone like clockwork, too, Britt feared, shame burning her cheeks as she recalled the abandon with which she had kissed him. By the time she returned to Paris she would have been hopelessly under the spell of his charms and spending her time anguishing over why Philippe hadn't called, why he didn't get in touch with her. Finally she would have seen on the society pages the account of the masquerade ball and the subsequent announcement of the forthcoming marriage. Probably then she'd have jumped from the Eiffel Tower!

But Margo had saved the day.

According to what she had disclosed at dinner, the friends she had hoped to meet in Nice had gone on to Rome.

"The place was deadly dull," Margo had announced languidly over dessert. And anyway, why should she stay there when she could be here at the chateau with "her darling Philippe"?

Britt lay down and pulled the sheet to her chin.

Darling Philippe.

How stupid of her to have hoped, even for a moment, that the Fates might have had in store for her a god. With clay feet, she reminded herself, but a god nevertheless. She recalled how Philippe had looked when he approached her in the hall this afternoon, how his lips had seared hers in the study, the way his arms had molded her to his body. . . .

She pushed her wet face down into the pillow. It was business as usual tomorrow, and for a few days longer. Then home to Sydney—as ordinary a person as herself and the only likely candidate for the man in her life if she but had the courage to accept the truth. The career she planned at *La Revue* had no real substance. She recognized it now only as a ploy to tide her over until she was ready to face up to the fact that her life would never be a romantic, love-filled adventure, the beginning of which she had been expecting since she was no more than seventeen and still minding Aunt Tillie's shop.

The facts were that life in the golden autumn of Southern France sparkled with the colors of the rainbow. For Philippe and Margo and others like them, she reflected wistfully, it held all the gloss and glitter of kings and queens.

But for Britt Ryan of 12 Rue de Mont it would always print out on sleazy paper and only in plain black and white.

Chapter 7

Britt rose early the next morning, and after breakfasting alone in a sunny little room filled with potted marguerites and trailing ivy, she went directly to the large reception room beyond the entry hall to begin photographing an impressive collection of Breton antiques.

Her last resolve before falling asleep after hours of tossing had been to stop feeling sorry for herself. Life gave of itself to those who gave of themselves, and withheld from those who grumbled and growled about their lot. She was done with that sort of behavior, she decided. The thing to do was to get her work done here as quickly as possible, arrange an interview or two with Philippe when she was sure Margo would be present as well, and then return to Paris.

At breakfast she had formed a plan for the article she must write to accompany her photographs and had settled on which rooms and objects would best illustrate the grandeur of the chateau.

Now following her planned course, she leaned closer

to a carved curio cabinet and fixed her camera's sights on a delicate porcelain pitcher on a shelf inside. But just as she was ready to snap the shutter, a shadow fell over the pitcher and spoiled the shot.

Whirling in disgust, she found herself face to face with Philippe. His appearance indicated he had slept as poorly as she. Not even his tan could conceal the pallor of his drawn face.

"I have to see you," he said through tight lips.

She lifted her chin saucily. "Well, here I am. Have a look."

He grabbed her arm roughly. "Not here. Come into the study."

She dug her heels into the thick pile of the carpet. "I've seen the study, thank you. There's nothing there I care to photograph."

"We can't talk here."

"That's quite all right. I've nothing to say anyway."

His jaw muscles leaped to ridge his cheeks. "Then you can damn well listen to me." With superior force he pulled her stumbling toward the study and shut the door behind her.

"Sit down."

Her green eyes glared icily. "My, my, another display of your lovely manners."

He took a seat on the sofa and jerked her down beside him. "The first thing I have to know is whether you meant it when you shrugged off as meaningless what happened in this room yesterday."

"You mean Margo's call?" she said with manufactured innocence.

"I mean our kiss!"

"You have your nerve asking me that after all I heard at the dinner table."

His dark eyes sparked with a primitive fire. "You do care. It meant as much to you as it did to me."

Her lip curled. "In other words, nothing."

He jerked her to him. "I want you to promise me something. Promise that you won't close your mind to anything, not *anything* for the next couple of days."

His nearness made breathing difficult. "What do you mean?"

"I mean that I have to work things out." He took her hands in his. "I can't just throw over everything all at once, but I promise you, if you'll just be patient—"

What was he saying? That there was hope for the two of them after all? Britt's heart began a slow thudding.

"You see," she heard him saying, "Margo didn't come back from Nice because no one was there to entertain her. She came back because she found out you were here."

Britt blinked. "How could she have done that?"

He gave a harsh laugh. "She has her methods, and I'm just beginning to discover the extent to which she'll go to have her way."

"Are you saying the things she said last night aren't true?"

He put his arms about her and spoke against her cheek. "I'm saying they aren't final." His hands moved down to her hips and she subdued a wild urge to lift her lips to his.

"What if Margo should come in now?" she whispered.

"She won't," he murmured hoarsely. "She always sleeps until noon."

A surge of rage swept over Britt. She shoved him back and came off the couch. "You're really too much, do you know that? Playing both ends against the middle and brazen enough to think you'll win!"

He leaped up. "Why are you so angry?"

"Why wouldn't I be? Do you think I'm a complete idiot? How neatly you've worked things out! Day or night one or the other of us—Margo or I—will always be on tap!"

"It isn't like that at all!"

"Margo lives here, doesn't she?"

"Yes, but—"

"You're engaged to her, aren't you?"

"Don't get hung up on that! There's so much more you don't understand."

Britt glared. "Are you engaged to her or not?"

He released a sigh. "Yes. I am."

Britt all but reeled from the simple admission. For a few brief moments when he had had his arms about her, she'd almost believed that Margo had lied and the answer to the question she had finally made herself ask would be no. Her legs threatened to give way, and she caught hold of a high-backed chair to steady herself.

"I think you're despicable." Her voice as well as her legs was trembling, but she went on relentlessly. "You're the worst kind of bounder—using your looks and your money." Her eyes swept over the room. "Using this house to feed your pleasures. I'd pity Margo for the life you'll lead her except that she's asked for it, moving in here with you, and for all her fine ways, living more commonly than any back street girl in Paris."

White-lipped, he regarded her. Finally he said in the same caustic tone he had used to refer to his mother, "And I pity you for your self-righteous bigotry, Britt Ryan. I hoped when I kissed you—" He lifted dark brows. "When *you* kissed *me*—that at least a little of my wickedness rubbed off."

In two strides he crossed the room, and when after a minute she moved unsteadily into the entry hall, he seemed to have vanished into thin air.

Determinedly Britt went back to photographing the

porcelain pitcher, noting the fine edge anger put to the work. Each time the brooding face of Philippe Dolman interposed itself, she clamped her jaws together more firmly and gave her whole attention to making that particular shot the best so far. When this article ran in *La Revue,* she vowed grimly, it had to be the most stunning pictorial essay ever produced. Nothing short of that would satisfy her rage.

But toward noon, her spirits flagged and when she stopped to change film, she set her camera down and leaned wearily against a marble column. Anger was the most exhausting of emotions, she thought dejectedly. Joy put wings on one's feet; love could lift one to the heavens, but fury— She sighed. Fury only made one ill.

Suddenly a cheery voice brought her to attention.

"Ah, there you are. Miss Ryan, isn't it?"

A squat little lady of seventy or so was approaching from the study. "I was assured you were somewhere on the ground floor." She extended her hand. "I'm Martinique LaSalle. I'm sorry I wasn't about to greet you last night." She smiled warmly. "That's one of my duties, you know, but I was away on a short vacation." She drew in the corners of her mouth, changing her smile to a wry grin. "Quite short, in fact."

Britt took the pudgy little hand. "How do you do?"

"Have you had your lunch?" Bright blue eyes snapped. "I suspect not, nor morning coffee either."

Britt laughed. "Do I look so dreadful?"

"Not at all. Only thoroughly exhausted. Photography must be quite a tedious task." She made a clucking sound. "You career girls. I don't know how you do it."

"Neither do I." Britt felt herself relaxing in the company of this sympathetic lady whom she took to be the housekeeper. "I'm not a career girl actually."

"Oh? My error. I understood you came in Mr. Fernham's place for *La Revue.*"

"That's true, but I'm only filling in for my friend. This is not my regular job."

"I see." The round little eyes disappeared into soft folds of flesh. "Then come and rest awhile. We'll lunch together, and you can tell me what you think of the chateau."

Over *coq au vin* and a plate of delectable fruits, Britt spoke of her morning's discoveries and received from Martinique LaSalle some helpful suggestions for focusing the article around the period pieces collected by the Dolman family through the centuries.

"That's a marvelous idea," said Britt, immediately discarding her own plan for the superior one of Madame LaSalle. "You're so familiar with every aspect of the chateau, you must have been with Monseiur Dolman for quite a long time."

The round little face crinkled with delight. "I put on his first diapers. I'm his aunt, dear child. Didn't you know that?"

Britt blinked. "Why, no."

"I suppose I assumed Philippe had spoken of me, or—" Her smiled dimmed, "that Margo had. You did meet Margo?"

Britt nodded.

"Lovely girl," said Madame LaSalle without enthusiasm. "Though somewhat unpredictable."

Britt agreed silently and sipped her wine. The less said about Margo St. Croix the better, she thought. Once away from this place she hoped never to think of her again. "Do you live nearby?" she asked, setting aside her glass.

The woman laughed. "On the second floor, my apartment adjoins Margo's. But the chateau is not my home, actually, Just before his death, my husband and I bought a cottage near the Spanish border, but I'm able only to vacation there from time to time, though I hope one day not too far hence—" She let the words trail away, then picked them up at another point. "I was at the cottage last night, as a matter of fact. I had intended to stay another fortnight, but when Philippe called to say that Margo was returning, of course I had to come back at once."

"I'm afraid I don't understand," said Britt, though with a sinking heart, she was beginning to.

"As I said Margo lives here too, in the apartment adjoining mine. She has ever since she left school. Because we're distantly related and because during Philippe's boyhood I made the chateau my home, I was the natural choice to serve as chaperone."

Britt's lips parted. "You're related to Margo? Then Philippe and Margo are kin."

Martinique laughed. "By no more than half a dozen drops of blood. They're something like sixth cousins, but their fathers were quite close as boys and continued that relationship through their business and social dealings for the remainder of their lives. They died together actually, in an automobile accident near Monte Carlo. Margo was fifteen, in school in Switzerland.

"Her mother had died years before and Henri—Philippe's father—was to be her guardian in the event anything happened to her own father before she came of age. The responsibility fell of course to Philippe."

Britt was aware of making an appropriate remark, but she was too stunned by what Martinique LaSalle had said to know what it was. She could only hear with ringing clarity her own dreadful accusations of the early morning, none of which it appeared now had the slightest basis in truth.

"Naturally it would have been unsuitable for Philippe and Margo to live alone in the chateau, so I was summoned, and I've been here ever since, though I will say—thanks to Margo's penchant for the jet set, as she calls it—she's often away for weeks at a time, and I'm free to go home then. I can't understand why she decided so suddenly to come back last night. Nice is her favorite spot this time of year.

"Of course," the woman babbled on, "since she and Philippe are to be married—" A plump hand came out and covered her mouth. "Oh dear, now I've said more than I've a right to."

"Don't worry," said Britt woodenly. "Margo told me of their engagement herself."

Relief cleared Madame's troubled brow. "Then you know about the ball too?" She sighed contentedly. "It's to be a sumptuous affair. I'm really quite surprised Philippe agreed to it at all."

"What do you mean?"

"He's such a private person, my nephew. Though he values the chateau and everything in it, he considers the place his home, not a showcase." The bright eyes fixed themselves upon Britt. "I'm a little surprised that he's allowed even your article. Or was that Margo's idea too?"

"I hardly think so," said Britt drily.

"Well, I suppose now that he's to be married, it's just as well he's had a change of heart. Margo will never be content unless she's constantly entertaining." The sun left her smile. "Poor Philippe," she murmured. "I wonder if he knows what he's letting himself in for."

Poor Philippe indeed! Britt hid the turmoil of her emotions behind a mask of calm. He could have told her Martinique LaSalle lived here! For the second time he had led her into a trap and let her snare herself with her own words. She had half a mind to pack up her things this moment and get away as fast as she could. It seemed the longer she stayed, the bigger fool she made of herself, though how she could top her angry words to Philippe this morning, she had no idea.

"Margo's coming home so suddenly," Britt heard Madame LaSalle saying, "has spoiled Philippe's surprise for her too."

"Oh?" Britt wished she could terminate this luncheon before she was provided another disturbing insight into Philippe Dolman's life. "What kind of surprise?"

"He's having the apartments in the east wing completely redecorated. He's always preferred the south wing himself, but Margo was so opposed to living there after the wedding—it's so removed from everything, you know—that he finally gave in to her. But she wasn't supposed to know that he had done so until just before the ball. That's why he accompanied her to Majorca for a month before she left for Nice. He thought the two journeys combined would allow ample time to complete the work, but she's such a little snoop—" Madam broke off and smiled apologetically. "I daresay she's on to the entire scheme by now."

So the redecorating was the project he had spoken of, not herself at all. And if he had been in Majorca for so many weeks, it was little wonder Sydney had had difficulty contacting him. She had been mistaken about so many things concerning Philippe that he must think her a terrible fool. "Perhaps Margo hasn't awakened," she said lamely. "I understand she sleeps until noon."

"Ordinarily. But she was up before nine this morning."

Then she could have come into the study, Britt realized with a tremor. How would Philippe have handled that?

"She's out riding with her groom-to-be," said Martinique with a touch of irony.

Britt had a quick picture of Philippe reaching out to

Margo instead of herself, lifting Margo onto his horse. So much for fantasies! And for love at first sight and all the other stupidities in which she had indulged the last few days. A little shudder seized her, and she pushed back from the table. "The lunch was lovely, but I ought to get back to work."

Martinique LaSalle put out a warm hand. "You were wonderful company. It's so refreshing to have a willing ear to chat into. Men are so impatient with women's trivial talk, and Margo—" Madame LaSalle drew herself up resolutely. "Never mind. I've said quite enough about Margo for one day. I'm sure you're already thinking I'm overcritical of my charge."

"Not at all," answered Britt, feeling a bit sorry for the dumpy little woman and for Margo too. Obviously they had quite different views of life and must chafe each other badly. "It won't be long before you'll be relieved of your responsibility and can go back to enjoying your view of the Pyrenees."

The other woman gave her a wistful smile. "I won't deny I'm dreaming of the day."

Chapter 8

Much to her relief, Britt was able for several days to avoid all but mealtime contact with Philippe and Margo. On the day following her luncheon with Martinique LaSalle, the costumers arrived from Paris with finery for the ball. Fittings occupied Margo, and Philippe took advantage of her preoccupation by overseeing the decorators.

The next day the two of them spent both morning and afternoon preparing for the Limoges meet, and on the third day Britt herself found occasion to be absent from the chateau.

She was in need of delivering some of her film to the photographer in Perpignan who had agreed to process it, and when she learned that Martinique was driving into town, asked if she might accompany her.

Martinique was glad to have company and throughout the drive chattered almost constantly on a variety of topics. Britt had already discovered Philippe's aunt to be an invaluable source of information concerning the furnishings of the chateau as well as its history, and she was eager to hear anything which would cut short the inevitable interviews she must conduct with Philippe before the assignment was complete.

But at least he had made no further reference to the daily inquisition he had first planned to submit her to. Probably because such meetings were no longer appropriate. Margo had returned, and whatever amorous adventures Philippe had been considering, he had now abandoned.

While Madame LaSalle chattered on, Britt let her own thoughts dwell briefly on Margo. Despite an inclination to dislike the girl, Britt had to admit that Margo seemed to be exerting every effort to be pleasant. Whenever they met, Margo had a ready smile, and though once or twice Britt had wondered at its sincerity, still there was no denying the girl's graciousness.

Why, Britt wondered, did Philippe question her excuse for cutting short her visit in Nice? And what had he meant when he said she had her methods for finding out what went on at the chateau in her absence? Did one of the servants do spy duty? But that was out of the dark ages! Britt glanced across at the woman behind the wheel. Certainly the informant could not be Martinique who seemed barely able to conceal her distaste for her charge.

But if Philippe's suspicions were true and Margo had returned because of Britt's presence, then that fact cast an entirely different light on Margo's motives as well as her behavior. It would appear either that she was skating on thin ice with Philippe and recognized the necessity of constant vigilance, or that she was simply a jealous-natured person. Or— Britt sighed. Perhaps the truth lay somewhere between the two.

"Tired?" said Martinique with a sympathetic smile. "I shouldn't blame you, you've been working so steadily the past few days."

"I want to get finished," said Britt.

"Well, I'm glad you've decided to take this day off at least. Will you be able to find enough to occupy your time until four?"

"Oh yes. Perpignan's a fascinating place. If I run out of things to do, I can always sit by the river."

Martinique pulled up at a corner on the main thoroughfare. "Shall I drop you off here then?"

Britt got out. "Where shall we meet?"

"This same spot?"

Britt nodded in agreement and waved her off.

The photographer, whom Britt sought out first, promised to have her work completed shortly after three, so with nothing special to do until that time, she found herself assuming the relaxed pace of the citizenry and wandering happily through the little shops lining the streets.

In one she purchased a card to send to Sydney, and in another some small native crafts for other friends in Paris. An autumn haze cast a golden glow over everything it touched, and for the first time in days a sense of peace stole over her.

By lunchtime the walk had stimulated an appetite, and Britt stopped at a sidewalk cafe for an omelette and fruit. Then for an hour she was content simply to sit and watch the passing crowds.

Gradually, however, thoughts of Philippe intruded on her tranquil mood. How nice it would be, she reflected wistfully, if she could turn back time to the morning the two of them had started out for the chateau. If only she had behaved differently on that ride!

Yet what real change would it have made if she had? Philippe would still be engaged to Margo. That—not a few careless words in a lemon grove—was the true stumbling block in their relationship.

But what good did it do to look back? There was no way she could alter anything that had happened to her since she came here, and even if she could, did she really want to? Philippe was still as arrogant and rude and caustic at times as he had been the first evening they met. Not at all the kind of person she could envision herself spending a lifetime with.

But on the other hand, she could not deny there was that about him which held an almost overpowering appeal for her. His unexpected moments of gentleness . . . an undercurrent of strength which he kept on a tight leash . . . and—most disturbing of all—the naked yearning he displayed for her whenever they were alone.

Now in the sunlight of the sidewalk, her imagination conjured up again the warm male scent of his skin when he had held her in the study. She felt again the tanned smoothness of his cheek against hers—his hands moving over her body.

She stood up suddenly. What kind of fool was she, to go on reliving a dead dream? The moment she heard of his engagement, she should have put all thoughts of Philippe Dolman out of her mind.

Now she would, she decided with determination.

She would walk over to the hotel terrace, order an ice, and concentrate on the beauty of the afternoon. Soon enough she'd be back in the hustle and bustle of Paris, and she'd be grateful enough then for a lovely memory of this drowsy afternoon in Perpignan. Why mar it with frustration and sad thoughts?

Striding along purposefully, she soon reached the hotel, and settling herself at one of the little tables, set aside her purchases and placed her order with a smiling waiter.

But she had barely begun on her ice when, looking up, she saw to her dismay, a familiar figure approaching the table. *Philippe!*

Her heart came up in her throat. "What are you doing here?"

Without greeting, he pulled out a chair and sat down, eyeing the dish in front of her. "I was famished for a strawberry *granite* the same as you." He flashed a smile at the waiter. "And a glass of Perrier, please. Perrier, Britt?"

"No, thank you," she answered stiffly.

When the waiter had gone, Philippe cleared his throat. "Where have you been?"

"I had some business to attend to. Then I went shopping."

His glance moved over her packages. "I can see that. But I'm more interested in where you've been for the past several days."

"At the chateau, of course. You've seen me."

"Only at mealtimes."

So he'd noticed! "I've been busy. So have you, I believe."

Taking his cue from her, he spoke in a detached manner. "Is your work going well?"

"I should be finished by the middle of next week if the shots I'm having printed today turn out as I hope."

His tanned fingers toyed with a folded napkin. "You sound eager to leave."

"I am rather."

A silence fell over them. The waiter brought Philippe's ice, and they ate to the accompaniment of small metal spoons clinking against the sides of their dishes.

Finally Britt said carefully, "I'd like to apologize to you. I misjudged your relationship with Margo. I spoke rashly and what I said was in poor taste. I hope you'll forgive me."

He leaned back and looked at her. "A proper little speech," he murmured. "Quite properly delivered."

Her cheeks burned. "You're infuriating," she said from between clenched teeth. "Do you know that?"

His gaze held steady. "Yes, I know that."

"You work at it, don't you!"

His smile was caustic. "I don't have to, unfortunately. It's almost a reflex."

"Why did you sit down here? Just to spoil my afternoon?"

"I wanted to see you, and there never seems to be an appropriate time to meet at the chateau."

His voice had lost its bantering note, and for the first time Britt noticed how lustreless his gaze was.

"I'm generally about," she said in a less hostile tone. "You should have mentioned at dinner last night that you wanted a meeting."

He moved his glass of Perrier in a slow circle on the tablecloth. "The kind of meeting I hoped for," he said softly, "I wouldn't care to mention in front of others."

She shoved her dish away. "Really, Philippe!"

At the use of his Christian name, his head came up. In a low, carefully controlled voice he said, "I want to hold you in my arms again. I want to kiss you."

"You're engaged to Margo!"

"Do you think I don't know that?"

"Then what you're saying is indecent!"

"Wanting you the way I do is indecent."

Britt's lungs squeezed shut, and she started up from the table. "I won't sit here and listen to this."

His hand came out and caught her arm, his eyes voicing their own command. "Let me stay this close to you. For a little while at least."

Trembling, she sank back into her chair. "There isn't rhyme or reason for your behavior. In less than a month you're announcing your engagement. If you're not in love with the girl, why are you marrying her?"

"I never considered love when I asked her."

Britt stared. "You can't mean that!"

His strong chin jutted stubbornly. "But I do mean it." His eyes moved over her face. "I'm not even certain I love you."

His bluntness struck her like a blow. She stood up, her chair tumbling backward. "Well, there's certainly no question in *my* mind! I'm quite sure you don't!"

Again he caught her arm, his smoldering gaze still fixed upon her. "But if I don't, then why am I constantly thinking of you?"

"Let go of me, please!"

"Britt—" He got to his feet. "I have to know how you feel about me."

"Why?" she answered in a strangled voice. "Is that part of the challenge?"

His iron grip closed around her wrist. "I don't know what it is. That's what I'm trying to discover before it's too late."

"Before you're married, you mean?" she said bitterly. "Perhaps if you're that much in doubt you'd better call the whole thing off."

"I've considered doing that—and I will if I can be sure what I'm feeling for you has substance, that it's more than some stupid game my ego is playing with yours."

She struggled to free herself. "I haven't any idea what you mean by that."

His grip tightened. "When you kissed me—was that a game? Were you only playing at passion?" Now his eyes were unnaturally bright. "You admire the chateau, I know. And you can't be all that fond of Paris life—"

She broke free with the sheer force of fury. "You think I'd try to win your affections so I could be lady of the manor? So I could move up the social ladder? If so, you're right to worry about ego! Yours is all-consuming, Monsieur Dolman!"

"How can we solve anything, Britt, if you always blow up?"

She glared, white-lipped. "I don't have to solve anything! It's you who are in a quandary."

"I have to know if you care for me."

She gasped. "Do you know what you're saying? You're asking me to tell you that I love you so it'll be worth your time to go off in some corner and try to make up your mind whether you love me! Well, that problem I *can* solve. I don't love you. I don't even *like* you!"

Whirling, she ran blindly down the steps leading to the street. She heard him call her name, aware that the only other couple on the terrace was staring, but she ran on heedless of where her steps were carrying her. Only one thing was important: to get as far away from Philippe Dolman as she possibly could—and as quickly.

Chapter 9

The minute Britt and Martinique arrived back at the chateau, Britt pleaded a headache. Martinique offered an old family remedy, but Britt declined it with a wan smile and begged her friend to make her excuses at dinner. Then she fled to her room.

Flinging herself on the bed, she thought gratefully that at least there was one thing good about being the only occupant of an entire wing. No one could hear her sobs.

All the pent-up anguish of the afternoon spilled onto the down pillows until at last, worn out and hiccoughing, she sat up again. Her dull gaze traveled over the room and fell finally on the packet of photographic prints she had tossed aside without even bothering to look at them.

No matter. Whatever their quality, they would have to do. She was getting out of this place tomorrow, pictorial essay or no. Sydney would simply have to put together what she gave him or toss it into the waste bin, whichever suited him best. She had made a terrible mistake coming here, and every minute she remained served only to compound her misery. If only she could leave tonight! But where could she go? Even Paris was not far enough removed.

She wiped her eyes and hiccoughed again. Why not go to Land's End then? Aunt Tillie was always begging her to come. Wasn't this the perfect time? She'd spend a fortnight or two there and then go up to London to find a job. Certainly she'd had enough of France. The French were too volatile, too unstable.

Philippe was volatile and unstable.

A fresh burst of tears choked her. What was all that nonsense he had spouted this afternoon about calling off the wedding? He hadn't the slightest intention of doing that.

But he had looked so weary, so genuinely baffled. How could a man as certain of himself as Philippe be so indecisive when it came to matters of the heart?

Nevertheless, there had been nothing uncertain about him the first time he had gathered her into his arms. He had known then exactly what he wanted. And yet—

Her breath caught. Hadn't he said—just before Margo rang—that perhaps they both ought to run. *In opposite directions!* So he'd been in doubt even then. He had tried to buy time with her, she remembered slowly. The next morning in the study he had wanted her to promise she would keep an open mind. What was it he had said? *There was nothing final about his plans with Margo.* In essence the same thing he had said this afternoon. He couldn't turn everything over all at once, he had told her, and asked her to be patient.

A bewildering array of sensations swept over her. She'd done nothing he'd asked her to do. Her mind had been closed from the start. She'd been anything but patient!

What if— Her heart began a slow pounding. What if he really were in love with her? But then he would know it, wouldn't he? She knew she was in love with him.

The admission rocked her. After all that had happened, surely her feelings had changed. But gradually she forced herself to acknowledge that they had not. She was still in love with him. Probably she always would be.

Then why hadn't she said so when he asked her this afternoon? What kind of foolish pride was it that always made her say the opposite of what she really felt? Perhaps that was Philippe's affliction too. Neither of them trusted the other enough to expose his own vulnerability.

She lay back on the bed. If only he were here now, she mused, she'd send all his doubts packing quickly enough. Her arms ached to hold him. Desire glowed hotly at her center. But she'd had her chance this afternoon, and she'd turned her back on it. There was little reason to hope she'd ever have another.

Evening fell slowly over the valley. From her window, Britt, freshly showered and wrapped in a thin dressing gown, watched the shadows of the chateau fill up the dales and hollows. She heard the faint call of a loon and the laughter of the servants floating up from the dining room as they cleared away the dishes.

Behind her on the writing desk lay the stack of photographs she had picked up in Perpignan that afternoon. After her bath she had studied them carefully, a warm glow of satisfaction growing in her as she examined each one. They were all excellent. The details of the Breton antiques stood out with superb clarity; the triple archway she had photographed at sunrise yesterday was even more impressive than she'd hoped.

But dearest to her heart were the first two shots she

had taken: the striped balloon suspended delicately before the turrets of the chateau with the blue sky as its background; and—even dearer—the photograph of Philippe on his horse.

Quickly she crossed to the desk. How sharply Sydney's fine lens had lifted Philippe from the distant meadow and captured him floating, like the balloon, over the fence. She brought the picture to her lips. This one she would not share with *La Revue*'s readers, she vowed. It belonged to her alone. No matter how far from this place she wandered in her lifetime, it would always have the power to call her back, even if only in memory.

A soft sound at the door brought her up sharply. A knock? Or was it her imagination?

The sound came again. Probably the maid with a tray of dinner Martinique had offered to send up.

But when the door opened, Philippe stood on the other side.

Catching sight of him, Britt felt her body respond as if he had touched her. She wore nothing beneath the flimsy dressing gown that covered her and was acutely aware that the last of the evening's light was outlining her every curve, but she had no power to move. None even to speak.

He stepped into the room and shut the door. "Your packages," he said quietly and tossed them on the bed. "You left them on the terrace."

She watched him cross toward her as if they were both participants in a dream. Some part of her sang, *he's come! he's here!*, but the rest of her was paralyzed.

Then she heard her name break hoarsely from his throat and found herself in his arms.

He covered her face with kisses, his hands moving over the diaphanous material of her robe, their heat penetrating the filmy barrier, his fingertips curving over the swell of her breasts. His muscled chest pressed hard against her, the taut lines of his body molded hers.

"Philippe," she moaned. "Oh, my darling, darling Philippe."

His embrace tightened, his mouth came down on hers. They swayed together, each discovering in the other's movement fresh starts of passion, new fires that blazed at every nerve's end.

At last, limp and trembling, they pulled apart and sank beside each other on the window seat. He brought her hands to his lips.

"I thought I'd never be finished with that interminable dinner so I could come and find you."

Britt fought her way back to reality. "After this afternoon, I wonder that you wanted to."

He groaned and pulled her to him again. "I had to hold you." His lips moved in her hair. "I had to hear you call me darling."

His skin against her face warmed her like fine wine. "You didn't know I would."

"I did." He gave a low laugh. "No matter what you said when you ran away."

Uneasiness stirred within her. "Perhaps it would have been best if you'd listened."

"I knew you didn't mean it, not when I looked at your face." He traced her cheekbone with a gentle finger. "That high color, those wonderful eyes—seas I've waited all my life to drown in."

"I was furious with you," she murmured.

"But now you're not." He kissed her again. The minutes ticked by on the ormolu clock on the dresser. Finally he released her, his face flushed, his eyes heavy-lidded. "I'd better leave, or I never will." But even as he spoke, he reached for her again.

She pulled away. "There's so much we need to sort out, Philippe." She swallowed. "There's Margo."

"Margo," he muttered. "I'd all but forgotten her."

"You're going to be married to her. You can't have forgotten that."

His eyes glowed darkly. "For the moment I had. You make me forget everything except how much I want you." He started to take her in his arms again, but she evaded him.

"I feel guilty meeting behind Margo's back. She's been friendly to me."

He laughed harshly. "You need to know her better."

She turned a puzzled gaze on him. "You never speak of her with tenderness," she said quietly.

"I never feel any."

"Then how can you plan to spend your life with her?"

A flush rose from his throat. "It's past time for me to marry. I thought she'd make a suitable wife."

Britt recoiled. "And now that you've changed your mind, you'll simply toss her aside?"

His lip curled. "No one ever tosses Margo aside. Tenacity is her strong suit, and once she has her claws in you—" He broke off. "I'll think of some reason to break it off with her. Some arrangement more advantageous to her than marriage to me."

Britt felt as if the blood in her veins had turned to ice. "What would that be?"

He shrugged. "Money—if the amount is large enough. A chateau of her own in a more desirable location." He brought Britt to him. "Don't worry. I can easily handle it though you'll have to be patient. It's bound to take time." His lips found hers, and he murmured against them. "But let's not think of that now. We've managed to steal a time for ourselves. Let's make the most of it."

Britt saw herself yielding to the pressure of his hard body against her own, welcoming his quick fingers loosening her gown—but simultaneously she was aware of another self pulling away, resisting.

"Don't," she said sharply. "We mustn't."

Frowning, Philippe lifted his head. "What's to stop us?"

Her heart hammered. "For one thing, you don't love me."

His sensuous mouth curved upward in a lazy, tantalizing way. "You're thinking of what I said this afternoon."

"Of course I am."

"Don't. Not now." His fingers caressed the back of her neck in a slow, hypnotic fashion. "Love," he murmured. "What is it? Is it the need I have for you, Britt? Is it the yearning that won't let me sleep?" His breath warmed her cheek. "Is it love that drove me here this evening, sick with wanting my arms around you? If that's love," he muttered hoarsely, "I've plenty of it, my darling—and more."

She stiffened in his arms. "It's none of those things."

His embrace tightened. "Then it's not important."

"I think it is."

"If we want each other—and you can't deny we do—" He kissed the hollow of her throat, the valley that divided her breasts. "That's all that matters."

"Not to me." She felt drugged, her legs had turned to water, her loins ached. But she went on resolutely. "I won't settle for less than love."

He seemed to find her remark amusing. "You can't even define it."

His words broke the spell. She pulled away. "It doesn't need defining. Love has a life of its own apart from flesh, apart from all the vagaries of the senses. It's guided by its own light, warmed from its own fires—"

"I'm fire enough for you," he said hoarsely and reached for her.

When she backed away, he flushed angrily. "I can't believe you'd throw away our chance to be together for some foolish emotion that exists only for romantics, for dreamers."

"It exists for me. And persists." Her eyes were bright with unshed tears. "Even while you stand before me and admit it's unreturned."

His brow furrowed. "Britt—"

He took a step toward her, but she whirled away and clutched the edge of the writing desk, her blurred gaze fixed desperately upon his photograph. "I wish you'd go now," she whispered.

"Britt, listen to me."

"Please!"

She stood stiffly, forcing herself to go on staring at the print while every fiber of her being strained after his receding footsteps. When at last she allowed herself to turn, the room had grown dark—and empty.

Chapter 10

Britt rose at daybreak after a sleepless night, dressed quickly and stole down for a last look at the garden's dewy freshness and at the valley below, dappled by the early sun.

What a beautiful place this was! No wonder Philippe had been appalled at her frivolous suggestion that it ought to be taken away from him and given to the French people. Knowing him as she did now, she felt if he were capable of love at all, it was the chateau and everything it stood for to which his heart belonged.

Not that she could blame him entirely, she thought casting a longing look at the craggy walls upon which wisteria almost as old as the stone itself clung tenaciously. There was a strength in this venerable building, an enduring quality which if it ever became a part of one's life would no doubt be as impossible to separate from oneself as breath or blood.

She shivered a little in the fresh morning air. It was good she was leaving. Another day or two and she would have fallen irreversibly under the spell of the place, a circumstance she could ill afford since after today she would share no part of the Chateau de Laon—nor any part of the life of its principal occupant.

With a sigh she turned her thoughts to matters over which she had a little control at least. There were still several areas of the chateau she wanted to photograph—an hour's work at the most. Then she planned to bid goodbye to Martinique and perhaps to Margo too, and be on her way. Just how she would manage to get into the village with her luggage was a problem she had yet to solve, but surely between now and noon someone would be going who would give her a ride.

A cool greeting came suddenly from the direction of the garden room, and turning, Britt saw Margo framed in the doorway. She wore a pale satin robe which clung seductively to her slim lines. Her hair was sleep tossed, her expression sullen.

"You startled me," said Britt with a smile. "I wasn't aware anyone else was up. It's very early for you, isn't it?"

"When one can't sleep," Margo replied curtly, "what point is there in lying in bed? Unless, of course, one isn't alone."

What was *that* supposed to mean? Britt wondered uneasily. And what had come over Margo? Was she always this ill-humored upon arising? "I'm sorry you had a restless night." She almost added that she'd had one as well, but under the other girl's scrutiny, she fell silent.

"Come inside," Margo commanded. "I want to talk to you."

Britt's heart stopped. Of course. This had to concern Philippe. But she had no desire to tangle with Margo over a matter that was already closed. In a few hours she would be gone from here. There was no need for a scene.

"I'm afraid I haven't time," she answered Margo as smoothly as she could. "I've some work to do before the sun gets any higher."

Margo turned on the path. "Damn your work," she said from between clenched teeth. "It doesn't mean a row of pins to me—nor to you either, I suspect—and I'm through with playing cat and mouse."

Britt spoke in a clear voice. "I don't know what you mean. I wasn't aware we'd been playing games."

"Oh, *really!*" Margo sneered.

Britt held on to her composure. "I thought your graciousness was quite sincere."

"I was willing for you to think that when it served my purpose. It no longer does."

"And what is your purpose, if I may ask?"

"I'm sure you don't need to, but if you're bent on carrying on with your naive pose, I'll be pleased to explain it to you."

With the feline quickness that characterized her every move, Margo flung open the door of the garden room and stalked inside.

Britt followed at a careful pace, her mind leaping ahead to anticipate Margo's accusations. Obviously she knew about last night. No doubt that was what had set her off this morning. But what else did she know?

Margo enthroned herself in a high-backed chair before the tea table and plunged immediately into the matter at hand. "Just what is it you have up your sleeve? You can't be silly enough to hope for marriage. Philippe would never demean himself to that extent." Her eyes narrowed. "Is it money? Is he paying you?"

The remark was so unexpected—and so farfetched! Britt almost laughed despite her shock. "You were going to do the explaining, I believe."

"In my own time I will. But first I mean for you to tell me how long you intend to stay here."

Britt caught herself on the point of revealing her plans, but the fat was in the fire now. If she could see how it burned without committing herself, what was the harm? "That depends," she answered mildly. "Why do you ask?"

Margo said without hesitation: "Because now *I'm* making the rules. Point one, for however long you stay you are not to be alone with Philippe. Not at all. Not for any reason.

"Point two," she went on. "Don't think you can meet secretly again. I know he was in your room last night. I know you've met privately with him in the study. And even before I left Nice, I knew you were planning to sleep here."

Britt had had enough. "Hold on! I came here to do an assignment for a magazine. That's *all* I'm here for."

"That might have been your original intention," Margo purred, pleased to have riled her adversary. "But you made the mistake of falling in love with your subject, didn't you?"

Britt flushed. "Are you telling or asking?"

"I don't have to ask!" Margo shot back. "It's written all over your silly face every time you look at Philippe."

Britt's cheeks flamed. "It occurs to me," she countered, "that if you have to spy on your fiancé, your position is terribly insecure."

The remark hit home, but Margo was quick to score a comeback. "Philippe's no saint. Like any other man, he'll take what he can get. It's my business to see it's not offered."

Britt yielded to an irresistible urge to puncture her conceit. "How do you know it hasn't already been?"

Margo bared white teeth. "Because I know Philippe.

When he's on the prowl, he's restless as a tiger, wretched, edgy. He was beside himself when he came down last night." Her hollow laughter filled the little room. "Don't worry. If it had happened, I'd know."

Britt was appalled at herself for allowing Margo to believe she would encourage a sexual conquest, but she had gone too far to back out now. "Knowing is one thing," she taunted. "Doing something about the next time is quite another."

Margo responded like a steel trap set to spring. "You let it happen, and I promise you I'll bring this chateau crashing around Philippe's ears. He'll never recover from the damage I'll do. Make no mistake about that."

Britt felt her blood run cold, but she managed a jaunty reply. "You haven't that kind of power."

"Oh, haven't I?" Margo spat back. "Try me and see."

Shaken, Britt stood up. "You don't frighten me, and I'm sure if Philippe heard you, he'd only laugh, but it doesn't matter anyway. I've finished my work. I'm leaving before noon." She paused, savoring her moment of triumph. "So you see, Margo, you've revealed yourself in all your ugliness without cause. In another few hours I would have gone away from here remembering you as the gracious, lovely mistress-to-be of the Chateau de Laon—not as the cat you really are."

But instead of the spiteful response Britt expected, Margo leaned back with a relaxed, somewhat thoughtful smile. "What a surprise," she said in a buttery tone. "You're so much smarter than I gave you credit for being."

Miffed, Britt could only respond: "I suspect you underestimate most people."

Ignoring the remark, Margo held on to her pleased expression. "I was almost certain you'd stupidly bow your neck and sputter about for a while longer. But for you to capitulate immediately—that's quite amazing. I congratulate you."

Britt caught her breath. "I am not capitulating! My decision to leave was made yesterday afternoon. It has nothing to do with what you've said."

Margo smiled lazily. "Have it your way. You're going. That's all I care about."

Britt had half a mind to change her plans, but even if she bested Margo, there would still be her feelings for Philippe to subdue and that task she had neither the heart nor the strength for.

Holding her tongue, she drew herself up and without a glance at her antagonist, marched from the room, feeling very much the loser in a battle in which the forces against her had been overpowering from the start.

After her haughty exit, Britt found herself too badly shaken to photograph anything and decided instead to pack first and try later for the remaining shots.

But it took less than half an hour to gather her few possessions and make ready for her departure—far too short a time for her to have regained her composure. With a sigh, she set her bags outside the door in the hallway and rang for the houseboy to take them below.

At least one good thing had resulted in her flight from Margo. She had run headlong into the gardener loading his truck with flowers from the chateau gardens. At the sight of the masses of blossoms, Britt remembered that it was Philippe's practice to keep the cathedral in Perpignan supplied with fresh bouquets. She had made arrangements to leave when the truck did at mid-morning.

Consulting her watch, she saw she still had an hour and a half. If she omitted photographing the moat, which really wasn't particularly appealing, she'd have a little time to rest and say her goodbyes to Martinique and still be on hand when the gardener was ready to leave.

She turned toward the window, then halted, astonished by the scene it framed.

Across the way on a knoll, Philippe and a group of estate workers were inflating the red and white balloon.

For a moment the sheer delight of seeing the splendid contraption mended and being made ready to take to the air shut out all other thoughts. Then almost at once she realized that Philippe and Margo—whom she now saw crossing the grass toward him dressed fashionably in a tan and white blazer and pale pleated skirt—were about to set forth on a journey.

Her heart turned over at the sight of them together. Even from this distance, they made a striking pair. With their height and aristocratic bearing they were a regal couple. But it was all a sham. Neither really cared for the other.

Britt turned away, sickened.

But seeing them together had set going the recorder in her brain. Margo's vicious comments replayed themselves. In accompaniment, the tawny eyes, sharp as a leopard's, gleamed with malicious pleasure at the idea of having driven Britt away from the chateau. That was the bitterest medicine of all, particularly since it wasn't true. But if she had gone on trying to convince Margo of that, she'd have come away looking more like a fool than ever.

Still it was some consolation—though a tardy one—to realize that although Margo had pretended to be certain no intimacy had occurred between Britt and Philippe, she was not certain at all. She had given herself away at the very beginning by asking if Philippe were paying her. If she knew so much, she would not have needed to ask what Britt had had up her sleeve.

Despite the rawness left by Margo's insults, Britt found herself smiling. Margo was definitely running scared. And yet—

Britt's heart stood still.

There was something so terrifyingly calculated in the way Margo had said she would bring down the chateau around Philippe unless Britt desisted at once from seeing him. It was Margo herself who had a trick up her sleeve, Britt decided uneasily. But what was it? What could she possibly do that could harm Philippe? With his six-hundred-year-old name, he could hardly be more solidly established if he were the president of France! Probably this was only another bluff. Yes . . . surely it was. . . .

But still the cold thought persisted. What if it weren't?

Then she remembered with a start that none of this was any of her affair. *You're leaving, remember,* she chided herself.

By tomorrow at this time she'd be back in her flat on the Rue de Mont; by next week, on her way to England. Any part she had played in Philippe's life or in Margo's dramatics was over.

It was a little sad though, she thought, stealing another glance at the magnificent balloon bobbing in the morning light, that Philippe was to have no happiness in his marriage. Margo was a despicable witch. He'd never have a moment's true joy with her.

But perhaps Margo was to be pitied too, she countered stubbornly. What kind of husband would Philippe make if he were marrying her only because it was the right time in his life for him to take a wife? He'd admitted he felt nothing for Margo, and even a cat deserved to be stroked now and then!

Britt got up, concluding her ruminations by concocting a panacea: perhaps the truth of the matter was they both deserved each other! Let them fight it out for the rest of their lives if they chose. It didn't matter in the least to her.

Still— She paused on the threshold to look back at the elegant suite she was seeing for the last time. If, as she assured herself, she didn't care what happened to Philippe, why was her heart aching so?

Was she a fool for running away instead of staying and fighting for the only man she'd ever loved? Suppressed desire cracked the protective barrier of her hard won resolutions and flooded her suddenly with an intensity that shook her.

She wanted Philippe body and soul—and she wanted love too. Because it was all or nothing with her, she was settling for nothing. Walking away from the Chateau de Laon with only memories of a few stolen kisses when she might have had so much more if she'd been less proud.

She was denying some of her most basic human needs because of rigidly old-fashioned ideas that had been hammered into her as a girl and because of a foolish romantic notion that love was the only lasting foundation in a relationship between a man and a woman.

But at least one of them was in love. If Philippe were not, did it really matter so much? In the long run what difference would it make if it were only for a little while that the two of them were able to find joy, fulfillment and sexual satisfaction with each other? She was a grown woman now. Aunt Tillie wouldn't be scolding over her shoulder.

She sank weakly in an armchair, her head spinning. Thank God she was leaving. It wasn't only the chateau which had gotten into her bloodstream, but Philippe himself. He had the power, if he were to come through the door at this moment, to take her without a whimper. One kiss and her principles would topple like a row of dominos. Her cheeks burned with shame, but her titillated senses would not allow her to deny that now where Philippe was concerned, she was totally defenseless.

Chapter 11

When Britt entered the garden room where she had been told by a maid she would find Madame LaSalle at coffee, she was surprised to see Margo there as well.

The two of them exchanged brief glances, Margo accompanying hers with a smile. Evidently, Britt thought searingly, Margo had decided to resume her masquerade of friendship, at least in the presence of Martinique.

"Ah, here's Britt now," Margo said gaily to Martinique. "And just in time."

For what, wondered Britt. The chance to see Margo and Philippe, arm in arm ascending in the balloon?

Martinique set down her coffee cup with a clatter, her eyes round as marbles in her pudgy face. "You can't be serious about leaving today, Britt. Why, Philippe told me himself he hoped you could be persuaded to stay on for the ball."

A scowl replaced Margo's smile. "Oh, you know Philippe," she said crossly. "He bends over backward to be hospitable." Then remembering her role, added, "He doesn't understand that Britt's a career woman. She has to be about her work."

"Which is now finished," said Britt, turning to Madame LaSalle. "I thank you for having made my stay so pleasant."

"Oh, my dear, we've all grown so fond of you."

"Yes, indeed," purred Margo. "Quite fond."

Martinique started up suddenly from her chair. "Does Philippe know you're leaving? I think not. I'm quite sure if he did, he'd have mentioned it at breakfast. I'll just send one of the girls—"

"Please don't do that!" Britt said sharply, aware that she was pleasing Margo, but quite unable to do otherwise since just the thought of having to face Philippe had set her heart pounding.

"Perhaps Miss Ryan and Philippe have already said their farewells," said Margo softly.

Britt shot her a level look. "We haven't, but I'm sure you won't mind doing it for me."

"Not at all," Margo replied airily. "If it can wait until I return."

"Margo is on her way to Tours for a week," said Martinique. "And Philippe is off this morning for Lyon in his balloon." She fixed a sad-eyed gaze on Britt. "I'd hoped to enjoy your company in their absence. Now I suppose I might as well go on up to the cottage." She turned to Margo. "Though I hadn't thought of going until you and Philippe and the Rimbauds went to Limoges for the equestrian meet."

Margo spoke irritably. "It doesn't matter to me what

you do. We certainly don't need you at Limoges. As a matter of fact, if anything diverting is going on in Tours I may skip the meet altogether."

Britt, still recovering from her surprise that Margo and Philippe were setting out in different directions, took in this latest bit of information with a startled look which she tried to hide by bending over the coffee pot.

"You're not going?" said Martinique, as baffled as Britt. "But isn't Philippe counting on you for the team events?"

"He'll manage well enough. Or he can drop out of the competition if he can't. He doesn't care a flip for it anyway, and it's all deadly boring, if you ask me. Particularly the days afterward that we always have to spend on that wretched farm."

"Why, I love the farm!" cried Martinique.

"Then you go," said Margo curtly. "And speaking of going—" She turned to Britt. "You may ride with me as far as Tours. Rene is driving."

"No, thank you."

"Oh, but I insist."

Martinique frowned. "If she doesn't choose to, Margo—"

"I have transportation to Perpignan," said Britt.

"With whom?" snapped Margo.

Britt allowed herself a little smile. "The gardener. So you needn't worry."

Margo lifted her chin. "I won't. As long as you're properly taken care of." She paused in the doorway. "It was an interesting experience knowing you. I'll look forward to your article." Her lips curved scornfully. "If it comes out."

"Well!" Martinique stared at Margo's retreating back. "What a strange thing to say. What did she mean, Britt?"

But Britt was unaware that Martinique had even spoken, for just as Margo exited, the door to the garden opened, admitting Philippe.

He wore light tan trousers and a silk shirt that revealed temptingly his heavily muscled torso. In his hand he carried an unopened bottle of champagne, which he lifted now in a mock salute. "Anyone care to wish me a safe landing?" he said lightly, but his dark eyes were solemn as they rested on Britt's flushed face.

"I'm afraid you've missed Margo," said Martinique. "But Britt and I will wish you well, of course." She held up her cheek for a kiss. "Are you leaving soon?"

"I'm waiting on the wind," he replied, "but I suspect I can be off within a quarter of an hour." He turned to Britt, eyeing her neat twill suit and high heels. "Not your usual picture-taking garb, is it?"

"Britt's leaving us," said Martinique. "I wanted to send for you, but—"

"But I knew you were busy," Britt broke in crisply. "I saw the balloon from the window. I'm glad to see it's back in working order."

"So am I." He regarded her calmly, as if, thought Britt, what had passed between them last night was an illusion. "You've never had a close look at the balloon, have you? Why not come now, and I'll show you the gondola."

Blood poured into her cheeks. "Thank you, but I haven't time. I'm just going."

"With the gardener, I believe you said? Then you'll have plenty of time." Philippe took her arm and propelled her to the door. "He's still cutting chrysanthemums."

But I didn't say how I was going, Britt thought numbly. Had the gardener told him? "I wouldn't want to keep him waiting."

"Oh, go along," said Martinique. "You'll enjoy seeing the balloon, my dear. It's quite a spectacle."

As the door closed behind them, Philippe said sternly, "Thought you'd sneak away, did you?"

"I wasn't sneaking!"

"It's customary for guests to say goodbye to the host," he chided, though if Britt had had the courage to look at him, she'd have seen laughter lurking at the corners of his mouth.

"We said everything we needed to last night."

He had no reply for that, and they moved in silence toward the balloon, dancing now against its tethers in the rising wind.

"Come," said Philippe when they had circled the craft. "We've just enough time before the men are ready to release the ropes for you to see the interior. The view from the ground is only one aspect of ballooning. You have to get up into the gondola to get the real feel of the sport."

Britt hesitated. "I'm sure that's true, but—"

Philippe put out his hands to pull her up. "What you will see will make an interesting side note for your article," he insisted.

Despite her distress at being near Philippe again, Britt did very much want to stand in the golden basket. Something childlike within her had responded to the striped balloon dancing on the ends of its ropes, and finally she gave way to her fascination by grasping Philippe's hands and allowing him to haul her up.

It *was* thrilling!

Standing at the basket's rim and looking across at the chateau, she felt excitement explode within her chest, and laughed aloud in sheer delight.

Philippe beside her grinned widely and circled her waist with his arm. She seemed not even to notice so absorbed was she in this new adventure. "This is like something from another age!" she exclaimed.

"It is. Ballooning started here in France in 1783."

Britt clasped her hands together. "It's so thrilling simply to be standing here, I can't imagine how you bear it when you're actually afloat."

"Look behind you here." He turned her gently toward the center of the gondola. "You'll get an idea of what equipment is needed. Better still—" He cleared a spot on a bit of canvas covering the floor. "Sit down a moment and have a look up toward the balloon. That perspective will give you a clearer picture of its size."

She did as he suggested and then watched with interest as first he increased the heat in a hissing little furnace and then tossed a bulky canvas packet over the rim of the gondola.

"What are you doing?"

"We don't need that," he said. "Nor this one either, I think." A second packet followed the first.

"What is that you're tossing out?"

"Ballast," he said cheerfully. "Its absence will make the craft lighter. It's usually jettisoned during ascent."

Britt watched as three more bulky packets went over the side. "Are you overloaded?" she said, puzzled at his actions. "Is that why you're getting rid of some of them?"

"That's it exactly." His eyes sparkled, but Britt was too intent on studying the furnishings of the gondola to notice. "What is that little stove for?"

"It produces the hot air we need."

"Oh, of course. Well, everything seems ready for your take-off." She got to her feet. "If I'm not to be a stowaway I'd better—"

A sharp intake of breath cut off her words. To the left of her astonished gaze the chateau's south turret glided by. On the right the road to Perpignan wound beneath them like a ribbon through the valley. "We're afloat!" she gasped.

Philippe came up beside her. "My! How did that happen?"

"How will we get down?" she cried.

"Oh, don't worry. There's nothing to it really." He gave her a reassuring smile. "But since we're adrift, shouldn't we enjoy the ride?"

She tore her gaze from the fascinating panorama below her. "The gardener's waiting for me," she said distractedly.

"I daresay he's given up on you by now," Philippe murmured. "Look. There are some hikers waving."

Britt leaned over the side of the gondola to wave back. The countryside passing slowly beneath them cast its spell. She was totally enraptured.

Philippe's dark eyes rested tenderly on her flushed face. "Marvelous, isn't it?" he said after a moment.

Britt could only nod. Below them tile roofed houses drifted past. Sheep, like carved figures from a crèche, fed in the meadows. "Everything seems to be moving except us," she breathed, spellbound. "And the silence! It's not at all like being in a plane."

"The wind is our motor. We're moving at the same speed it is so there isn't any sensation of motion."

She turned starry eyes upon him. "Is this the way birds feel?"

He laughed. "I'll ask the next one that goes by."

Abruptly she moved to the other side of the gondola. "Oh, come and look! All the apple trees are upside down!"

Minutes later they floated over a town. Children on their way to school waved their book bags and shrieked joyously.

Britt waved back. "What place is that?"

"Mazamet, perhaps. Yes. There's the cathedral."

His arm came around her as he pointed. Their eyes met. The muscled portion of his upper arm fell solidly against her shoulder. Her heart pumped furiously.

"Shouldn't we be getting back?" she said in a small voice.

His gaze held her. "Do you really want to?"

Dry-mouthed, she nodded.

"But all you've done so far is look at the countryside. You don't even know how the balloon operates. What will you say in your article?"

She moved away from him. "It doesn't have to be a technical account." She could hardly speak her pulse was racing so. "*La Revue*'s readers don't look for scientific explanations."

"For your own information then," he scolded lightly. "Aren't you even curious?"

"Of course. But I already know about the ballast." She glanced around the gondola. "I was wondering, however, why you're not steering."

His white teeth gleamed. "Because I can't," he said disarmingly. "Except for climbing up or floating down, there's little I can do to maneuver the craft."

An incredulous look came over Britt's face. "Are you saying we can't turn around and go back?"

He laughed. "Not exactly."

"What does *that* mean?"

"It means if we really had to go back, I could make the balloon rise by turning up this propane burner which would add hot air to the balloon; or I could release some hot air and we would descend."

"But I don't want to go up or down!" Britt cried. "I want to go backward!"

"In order to do that," he went on patiently, "we would have to find air currents, either above or below us, that happen to be going in that direction."

"Then you'd better get started looking!" she said sharply.

"Must you really go back to Paris today?"

"My work at the chateau is finished."

She saw the slow rise of his chest. "You didn't answer my question."

"Yes! I have to go back to Paris today." If only he wouldn't look at her that way. If only the sky weren't so blue, and Philippe so near—

"Why?"

"You know why." Her eyes glittered with gathering tears. "Do you have to humiliate me every time we're together?"

In a swift movement he had her in his arms. "Humiliate you?" His lips moved against her face. "That's the last thing I want."

"Then don't touch me," she said brokenly. "Don't tease me when I've already told you how I feel."

He lifted her chin, and she saw his eyes filled with the naked longing that was always her undoing. "But I'm not sure how *I* feel," he answered hoarsely. "Shouldn't I have a chance to find out?"

She pulled herself free and fixed her gaze on a winding stream below. Beside it white cows grazed and tiny purple flowers dotted the grass. Floating along in the sky with Philippe beside her was like a dream. They would never be more alone—or further apart.

"Even if I wanted to stay," she said woodenly, "I couldn't. It's dangerous, Philippe."

He caught her to him again, his voice intense. "Dangerous? How could it be?"

"Margo threatened me. Or rather it was you she threatened through me."

"How? When?"

In a carefully controlled voice Britt repeated her

morning's encounter in the garden, omitting only the impression she had left with Margo of intimacy between herself and Philippe.

"She said unless I stopped seeing you, she'd bring the chateau down around your ears."

"There's nothing she can do to harm either of us," scoffed Philippe. "Or the chateau either, unless she's a mind to blow it up with dynamite, and I can't see that, can you?"

"She meant it, Philippe. If you could have heard her—"

"I've listened to her often enough to imagine what a show she put on. I've always excused her spiteful little ways as those of a spoiled child. They never amount to much more than temper tantrums."

"I think you underestimate her. She has someone spying on us."

"Not up here." He pulled her to the rim of the basket and pointed out over the valley where the balloon's shadow skipped along a sandy road. "Up here we're the spies. Look." He laid his cheek against hers. "If we had a pair of binoculars we could even see what that farmer's wife is cooking for lunch."

Britt laughed in spite of her anxiety. "If only all of life were this kind of voyage." She sighed and turned up her face to his. "No tumult, no noise. Just this silent drifting."

His mouth came down on hers, hungry, searching. His arms tightened about her. Her better judgment which demanded that she resist him slipped from her as earth's fetters had done, and she answered his need with her own, pressing her body to him, her heart leaping as she felt the pressure returned. If only they could go on together for the rest of time, she thought dizzily. Weightless, with no responsibilities except to each other, no destination except each other's arms.

Reluctantly Philippe released her. "I do have to get busy now," he murmured with a hoarse note of regret. "Look below."

She leaned out. "The river you mean? Which is it?"

"The Dordogne. That means we're nearly there."

Britt blinked. "Where?"

With a formidable hiss, hot air began escaping from the balloon. "The farm." He worked steadily, in a deft, skilled way. "Follow the river to your left. In a moment you should be able to see the walnut orchard. Then the house beyond it."

"Oh, yes! I see it. And dozens of people crowded in the meadow. They almost look like a welcoming committee."

"In a sense they are. They're the retrieval crew."

Britt turned to stare at him. "But Martinique said you were going to Lyon. Why aren't they waiting there to haul you in instead of here?"

He flashed a smile. "I don't always tell Martinique everything. Besides, what does it matter to her where I go?" He laid his arm across her shoulder. "Or whom I'm with?"

Britt felt a shiver of apprehension. "It matters to Margo."

"Forget Margo, will you?" He gave her a quick kiss. "I want you to enjoy the descent."

As lightly as a butterfly settling on a daisy they floated down into the meadow; whereupon the cheering crowd of men who had followed on the ground the aerial tracks of the balloon fell upon the gondola like a swarm of ants, and before Philippe had popped open the first bottle of champagne and handed Britt an overflowing glass, they had the ropes secure.

Philippe's smoldering gaze found her eyes above the wine glass. "We've landed in our own world now, darling. There are no Margos here, and for a week, no one has to know that we're here either." He lifted his glass. "To our happiness."

A dozen objections crowded Britt's lips, but bringing her glass to his in response, she denied them voice. A week, he had said. All to themselves.

Fate had given her a second chance to be all Philippe desired. What did it matter if afterward she found she'd made a mistake? She had the rest of her life for regrets, but only seven days to share with Philippe.

Chapter 12

Philippe's farmhouse on the banks of the Dordogne was the most charming Britt had ever seen. There was none of the austerity of the chateau, but still its thick plank walls exuded a sense of history and permanence. Topped with apricot tiles—the typical roof of this area of the Dordogne—it clung snugly to the sunny side of a hill. Surrounding it were fields of maize, carefully tended vineyards sloping down to the river and acres of venerable walnut trees.

Within, the main section of the house consisted of a combination hall and sitting room which Philippe referred to as the *séjour;* a small, but pleasant dining area overlooking a meadow speckled with white cows;

and a rambling old farm kitchen Britt fell in love with the moment she saw it. Up the wooden staircase leading from the *séjour* was a cozy bedroom with its own little fireplace, a bath and a tiny sitting room.

The remainder of the dwelling was made up of two angling wings, one containing several bedrooms and baths; the other, a study and game room replete with darts and billiards and on the walls a gleaming array of harness buckles which Philippe announced had been collected by his great-grandfather.

"Oh, it's wonderfully warm and welcoming," said Britt with a deep sigh of satisfaction as they concluded their tour. "But my favorite room is the kitchen." She returned to it and ran her hand lovingly along the gleaming wooden drainboard, polished by countless years of use.

Philippe came up behind her and lifting her hair, kissed the nape of her neck. "I'm glad you like it because you're going to have to do the cooking, I'm afraid."

"Really?" She turned and teasingly traced the cleft in his chin with the tip of one finger. "What would you have done if I hadn't come along?"

"Madame Londine, the overseer's wife, usually provides, but we don't want a third party popping in at the wrong times, do we?" He nuzzled her neck. "I'd rather eat beans from a can and be alone with you."

A mixture of delight and anguish shot through her. She had set herself an alien course in agreeing to remain here. Could she stay true to it?

"There'll be no canned beans, thank you," she said shakily. Removing herself from his arms, she opened a cupboard door. "But the cupboard is bare. I'll have to have provisions."

"Make a list." His eyes traveled over her. "While you're changing into something more comfortable, I'll take it over to the Londines' cottage and someone can fetch what we need from the village."

For the first time, Britt remembered her luggage. "Philippe! My clothes! They're in the gardener's truck. I haven't anything except what I'm wearing."

He gave her a slow smile. "You won't need many clothes."

She felt color rising hotly from her throat. "I'll certainly need something! What am I to do?"

Laughing, he took her in his arms again. "It just so happens one of the crew took your bags out of the gardener's truck while we were with Martinique and loaded them into the gondola. That's why I had to get rid of a little ballast before we could ascend. In fact, you were leaning on the largest of them—covered with canvas, of course—when you were asking about the propane burner."

"What a rascal you are! And so sure of yourself," she pouted. "How did you know I'd agree to your little adventure?"

He chuckled. "You didn't agree, if you remember. You were kidnapped. But short of jumping out of the basket, what choice had you?"

His warm skin against her cheek gave off a tantalizing scent of maleness, and she felt as if everything substantial in her life were giving way to a consuming desire. She took a deep breath to steady herself. "It was pure chance you caught me before I left."

He shook his head. "It was in the stars. Margo made quite a point of coming out to the balloon just to tell me you were leaving. With her, she said, but I doubted that. When I came in to check, I saw your bags in the gardener's truck and sent back for one of the men to fetch them." His lips moved over hers. "After that, the balloon did the rest. I remembered the way you looked up at it from the meadow that very first day. I knew you'd never be able to resist coming aboard if you were given the chance."

"But what happens," she whispered, "when Margo's spy notifies her that we're here together?"

"Though Margo doesn't know it," he said, letting go of Britt, "her spy was given the sack this morning."

"What!·Who was it?"

"That prissy little minx who served us tea the first morning you came. She must have gone straight away and called Margo in Nice. I'd been puzzling ever since Margo's return just why she came back so abruptly. Then last night when I was leaving you—" He paused, both of them remembering what had happened in Britt's room. "There that girl was, hovering by the door. She had a supper tray for an excuse, but everything fell in place when I thought it over, and this morning I sent her packing."

"Does Margo know?"

"She may by now. I'm sure the little snip went right to the telephone when my man delivered her in Perpignan, but Margo would have left for Tours by then, so the message is probably just catching up with her."

"She'll be furious."

Philippe shrugged. "Let her be. It's I who should be angry. The idea of using a man's own servant to spy on him, particularly if the man is one's own fiancé." Too late he realized that with his mention of Margo and marriage, he had introduced into their hideaway world an unforgivable intrusion.

Britt turned away. "I'd better make my shopping list."

With the groceries from the village, Madame Londine sent over quiche, piping hot from her own oven, and when Britt had tossed a salad from the fresh garden produce she found tucked in the basket of supplies, she was able to lay a tempting supper in the dining area of the *séjour*.

Philippe, who had changed to riding breeches and another of the soft shirts that showed off so well the solid strength of his chest and arms, had laid a fire in the cozy sitting room. When Britt brought in the tray of food, he opened a bottle of Bordeaux, and they sat down to eat.

The strain which his remark about marriage had created, had eased with their settling-in duties, and now Britt felt securely wrapped in an aura of warmth and wholeness.

My cup runs over, she thought, watching the shadows of the fire dancing on Philippe's beloved face.

Catching her eye on him, he leaned back from the table and said with a contented sigh, "Delicious!"

Britt smiled. "Thanks to Madame Londine. Tomorrow I'll cook you something delectable myself." Her green eyes sparkled. "An old Ryan recipe."

"Irish stew, I hope," he said with a twinkle.

She made a face. "How did you guess?"

"What else would one do with potatoes and carrots and celery and parsley?"

"Make chicken pie," she answered laughing. "I'll try the stew on Tuesday."

Together they washed the dishes and tidied up the kitchen. "Let's go for a walk down by the river," Philippe suggested.

Britt agreed quickly, relieved that the encounter she both dreaded and anticipated was to be delayed a while longer. When she came down from upstairs with a sweater, Philippe was standing with his back to the fire, a faraway expression clouding his chiseled features.

"A *sou* for your thoughts," Britt said lightly. "Or should I offer a franc in these days of inflation?"

He smiled a little and took her hand. "I was just thinking how swiftly this day has gone. Our week will be over before we know it."

"Oh, Philippe, don't!" she whispered.

"Never mind," he said quickly. "We'll make the most of it." He slid his arms around her and kissed the hollow of her throat. "After tonight, nothing can separate us."

Britt swallowed. "I hope the weather holds," she said irrelevantly, her pulse throbbing.

"It won't, I'm afraid." On the porch the sharp air bit into their skin and they could feel the moisture it held. "See the circle around the moon?" he said. "That means rain in three days, they say, but I doubt if it will hold off that long."

For an hour they strolled contentedly along the riverside. The valley was so still, Britt felt they were indeed in a world all their own, and her anxieties, which had been alternating with spasms of desire throughout the evening, dimmed in the night's calm silence.

She felt so right with Philippe beside her. She belonged here, and she belonged to him—or she soon would.

Her heart began a painful pounding. She imagined herself drawn close into his arms, his hands upon her body in a way she had never before been touched. Would she know how to react? Would her emotions express themselves naturally, so that Philippe would understand how dearly she loved him? Would he know that even deeper than her physical yearning there lay within her a core of caring far more enduring than passion? Was she capable of sharing that with him, or would she be so caught up in the tumult of the moment she would forget all else except the exquisite desire which racked her each time they kissed?

Philippe's touch startled her. "Ready to go in?"

She took a breath. "Yes."

Once they were in the house, however, Britt, dry-mouthed and trembling, clutched at straws. "Could we sit a while beside the fire?"

Amusement flickered briefly in Philippe's dark eyes. "Whatever you like." He took a seat on the sofa and pulled her gently down beside him. "Happy?" he said quietly when she was nestled against his chest.

She nodded, hearing his heart beating steadily beneath her ear.

"But a little frightened?"

"Not of you," she said quickly. "You mustn't think that."

He touched his lips to her temple. "There's no one here but me," he murmured.

"There's me," she said wistfully.

His low-voiced chuckle sounded in her ear. "You're always so serious," he chided.

And Philippe is not, an inner voice warned. *This is a game to him, one he's played often.* But at once she was penitent. No one could have been more thoughtful and tender than he had been this evening. Or more gentle and loving. She turned in his arms and lifted her face. "Kiss me, Philippe."

A muffled groan escaped him. He gathered her to him, his strong hands moving up her spine, into her hair, while his mouth found hers. Lying back, he pulled her across his body, his hands slipping down over her hips, returning to curl about her shoulder, to cradle her head.

Her inner tension dissolved like a wax candle under the heat of his kiss. A warm pool of passion spread in her loins.

"Britt," Philippe moaned thickly. "My darling, my sweet dear Britt."

All at once he shifted, rose, and swung her up in his arms. She clung to his neck, eyes closed tightly against pinwheels of lust whirling behind their lids. Dimly she heard the creak of the wooden stair, and felt their bodies rising even as her passion soared.

But suddenly her cheek met cool linen sheets and something snapped within her. She found herself struggling with Philippe's taut body poised beside her.

"No, Philippe! No!"

She shoved with all her might, the thrust carrying her own body back across the bed. In an instant she was up, hugging her shoulders, her eyes wide in the moonlight. "I can't. Oh, please understand, but I can't!"

Philippe, dazed, sat up. "My God. What kind of woman are you?"

She hurried around the bed and knelt, her arms clasping his knees. "Forgive me." She wept into the rough cloth of his riding breeches. "I thought only fulfillment mattered. I thought I could."

He pushed her aside. Still huddled beside the bed, she heard the sound of his boots descending the stairs, then the slamming of the front door.

She held her breath. In a moment he would come back. Take her in his arms, patiently, as if she were a child. He would tell her he understood, comfort her.

The chill of the house stole over her. The downstairs filled up with silence that moved relentlessly up the stairs. When it climbed to the bedroom under the eaves, Britt collapsed across the bed in a storm of hysterical weeping.

Chapter 13

Britt woke to the tantalizing aroma of coffee drifting up the staircase from the kitchen below. For a moment she lay still, staring up at the rough-hewn logs in the ceiling while the events of the night before slowly fell into place.

For what seemed like hours, she had lain taut, listening for Philippe's step, starting at every snap and pop of the house as it responded to the evening's lowering temperatures. But he had not returned.

At last she slept. Sometime later she had awakened, chilled, and reaching to pull the feather comforter closer around her shoulders, she thought she heard someone walking on the graveled path that led around the house. She had gotten out of bed then and padded to the window, but there was no one in sight. Thin clouds scudded over the moon, and the Dordogne lay silver in the crooked arm of the valley.

Now it was morning.

She sat up. Was Philippe making breakfast, or had he gone over and roused Madame Londine to come and do it for him? Filled with apprehension for what the day might hold, Britt was preparing to throw back the covers when she heard footsteps on the stairs. Snatching the comforter back to her bosom, she stared at the door.

In a moment she heard a gentle knock. When she called, "Come in," the door swung open and there stood Philippe with a breakfast tray.

"Good morning," he said evenly, nothing in his expression or his voice betraying the slightest emotion.

Her hand went up involuntarily to smooth her sleep-tousled hair. "Good morning."

Crossing to the bedside, he set the tray down on a table. "If you'd rather have tea—" he began.

"No, no!" She wet her lips. "This is fine. Lovely." Her eyes searched his face. "You were kind to bring it to me."

"Take your time with it," he said tonelessly. "There's no hurry to go anywhere. It's raining." He turned then and went out.

The coffee scorched Britt's throat, but she scarcely noticed. Nor was she aware enough of the flaky croissant melting on her tongue to wonder who had baked it or where it had come from.

Philippe had brought her breakfast.

He couldn't be too angry then, could he? Or was that simply the act of a civilized host, something he would have done for any guest, no matter how despicable? She nibbled listlessly at the roll. What had he been referring to when he said there was no hurry about going anywhere? Where did he think they would go? Yesterday he had made a big thing of the fact that they were alone in this isolated spot. Now he was talking about leaving.

Or was it she who was to go?

A coldness clutched her heart. That was it. The next move was up to her, and Philippe meant for it to be toward Paris.

She huddled miserably in the soft folds of the comforter. There was no way she could know the extent of the damage her abrupt refusal of him had caused last night. Certainly he had been furious enough when he left her, but now this— She glanced toward the breakfast tray she had set back on the table. Yes, it *was* a tender gesture, a reconciliatory one. He had had all night to reassess her actions, and he had forgiven her.

A slow rising joy spread in her veins. With light steps she moved across the room to the closet. Rifling through the meager assortment of garments hanging there, she chose a burgundy sweater she knew accented the green of her eyes and the creamy tones of her skin, and to go with it, a soft tweed skirt she had paid double for on Regent Street simply because she couldn't bear not to own it.

Satisfied with her appearance at last, she took the tray from the table and made her way carefully down the stairs to the kitchen.

Philippe was sitting at the round wooden table in its center staring into a cup of coffee, but at her step he looked up sharply. No smile of greeting changed his solemn expression.

Britt took a breath. "That was a smashing breakfast," she said with forced cheerfulness. "You must have risen early to make it."

"I didn't go to bed," he answered quietly.

"Oh?" She turned from the drainboard, her heart in her throat. "I'm sorry to hear that."

"Since I was up anyway, I walked to the village baker's and got there just as the croissants were coming out of the oven."

"But that's quite a long way, isn't it?" she said timidly.

"Three or four kilometers." He got up and took his coffee cup to the sink.

"Philippe— I'm sorry."

He made a sound that wasn't quite a laugh. "It doesn't matter."

"I think it does."

Suddenly his eyes blazed. "You're a bit late worrying about it."

"I didn't say I was worried." She struggled to control the quick anger his condescension had ignited. "I said I was sorry."

"Shall we go upstairs to bed then?" he said in a brittle tone.

"Certainly not! You're a beast even to suggest such a thing after what happened."

"Then why did you bring it up?"

"Oh, really! You're impossible. One can't even apologize without being the victim of your testiness."

"You've had your part in contributing to that."

"I said I was sorry!"

His sigh exploded in the quiet room. "Forget it, will you? It's wretched enough wondering how we're to get through this damned day without our raking up all of that again."

She drew herself up. "You can do as you please. I'm leaving, of course."

He regarded her with an indulgent smile. "And how do you think you're going to manage that?"

"The village is only three or four kilometers, you said. I walked further than that to get to the chateau from Perpignan."

"What do you plan to do in the village?"

"Catch a bus. I was on my way to Paris, you know," she added haughtily.

"The last time a bus came through Vincome it was

carrying Spanish refugees from the civil war. Contrary to what you must believe, in the provinces all roads *don't* lead to Paris."

Britt absorbed this morsel of information with mixed feelings. If, after all, she couldn't leave today, then she might find a way to make her peace with Philippe. Even if everything were over between them, it was important to make him understand she had not purposely teased him to the height of passion only to turn him away. But in his present mood he would listen to nothing. Perhaps then his worry that the day might be a long one was legitimate. And what about tomorrow? And tomorrow and tomorrow?

"What do you suggest I do?" she said. "Obviously I can't stay here the rest of the week. If you'd put your mind to it, I'm sure you could come up with an idea."

"If it weren't Sunday, I might," he said sullenly.

"Oh." Now she saw the problem. Tradesmen or farmers who might be going beyond the village toward Paris or toward some larger town with public transportation would not be traveling today. She looked about her with a sudden feeling of desperation.

For the next twenty-four hours they were trapped here.

"Well, since it won't be Monday for a terribly long time," she said with a briskness she was far from feeling, "I'll start helping the day pass by tidying up the kitchen." She pushed up the sleeves of her burgundy sweater. "Then afterward, I'll put on the stew, and if it's stopped raining by then, maybe we could go out and gather a few walnuts."

He looked at her with amazement.

"Well?" She glared back. "I'm certainly not going to sit around all day and watch you sulk. I'd rather scrub the floors."

Suddenly he burst out laughing.

It was Britt's turn to look amazed. "I don't see what's so funny."

"You wouldn't." He went on chuckling as he picked up a dish towel. "You never laugh at anything."

"That isn't true!"

"When have you laughed?" he challenged.

"Why—yesterday!" She gave him a triumphant look. "I distinctly remember laughing in the balloon—several times! And once or twice after that, I think." She frowned. "Let me see—"

All at once they were both laughing. With hot water to her elbows Britt washed the china cups and saucers and scalded the coffee pot. Then while Philippe watched in wide-eyed astonishment, she scoured the sink with a foul smelling powder she found beneath it, and whipped out the chopping board and set to work with a vengeance on the carrots and potatoes.

When the stew was bubbling on the stove and its mouth-watering aroma filling the downstairs rooms, she whisked upstairs and made her bed and straightened her room.

When she came down again, cheeks flushed, Philippe was reading contentedly by the fire while rain dripped steadily from the eaves.

"I thought this was chicken pie day," he said without looking up.

Her hand flew to her mouth. "The chicken! I completely forgot about it. And it won't keep." She wheeled around toward the kitchen. "I'd better set it to boil at least."

His calm voice stopped her. "I've already done it."

She whirled. "You? I didn't know you could even poach an egg."

"I'm quite a good cook," he said indignantly. "Have you already forgotten who served you breakfast?"

She crossed the room slowly and sat down in the

chair opposite him. In a soft voice she said: "You're very nice, you know."

He answered gruffly. "I'm glad you like me."

"I love you."

His startled eyes fixed luminously upon her. "Then why that god-awful fracas we had last night?" he murmured.

"Because I care too much," she said. "About everything. You, me. Tomorrow."

He leaned forward and took her hands in his as he had done on the hotel terrace the evening they met and traced her lifeline across one palm. "It says here tomorrow will take care of itself."

"But not if one spoils it with foolishness today," she whispered.

He kept his eyes on her hand. "What I wanted to share with you I wouldn't call foolishness."

"In the right context neither would I. I realize for some people last night would have been the right context. But not for me." Her voice dropped. "I didn't know that until it was almost too late."

He was quiet for a moment. "I think you did know it."

Her eyes flew to his.

"But you tried to push it out of your mind to please me. And *I* knew that." He paused. "And took advantage of it."

They stared across the space between them.

"So what shall we do now?" he challenged.

A smile began at the corners of her mouth. "Well," she answered in a small voice tinged with mischief. "We could always put on our rain slickers and gather walnuts."

Chapter 14

The morning passed so swiftly neither Britt nor Philippe would have believed it was noon when they came in from the orchard had it not been for their stomachs demanding to be fed.

The stew had simmered to a fine rich broth and the little chunks of succulent beef bobbing about in it melted in their mouths. Crusty croissants left over from breakfast and glasses of white wine, followed by a plate of black and white grapes Britt had discovered growing in a tangle at the edge of the orchard, completed the satisfying meal.

"Go and have yourself a nap, why don't you?" suggested Britt when she saw Philippe fighting back the third yawn.

It was plain the idea held enormous appeal for him, but he hesitated. "What will you do?"

"Oh, don't worry about me. I'll tidy up here." She stacked plates and bowls. "ThenI'll read or take a walk if the sun comes out." She smiled. "I'll be perfectly content."

Still he hesitated. "You're certain?"

"Of course. Why wouldn't I be in such a lovely place?"

"*I* always am," he agreed, "but—"

"But Margo isn't?" she finished for him.

"She hates it here. If we aren't playing backgammon or shooting billiards or planning for guests to come or drinking with those who are already here, she all but climbs the walls. I can't imagine her sitting down with a book or going for a stroll on her own."

Britt picked up the dishes. "We're quite different, Margo and I," she answered lightly.

"You are indeed," he murmured. He set a foot on the stairs, glanced up toward the bedroom where Britt had slept, and then turned abruptly and strode off toward the wing that contained the other bedrooms he had shown her yesterday.

She stood still, the dishes in her hands, until she heard the door of one of the rooms close. After their talk earlier, nothing further had been said about what had happened last night—nor about tonight. Philippe's choosing a separate room for himself was the first indication Britt had had that the evening to come might pass without unpleasantness. But already she had felt a new understanding growing between them as they had wandered in the orchard, filling a basket with nuts and taking shelter once in a sweet smelling hay shed when a deluge descended.

There Philippe had talked a bit about his childhood at the chateau where Martinique had assumed the maternal role after his mother's departure; and Britt told him what it was like to tend a tea shop when one could barely see over the counter.

She had found it easy to laugh in that relaxed atmosphere, and had noted what pleasure her gayer spirits seemed to bring to Philippe. It was obvious the farm meant a great deal to him and that when he was here some of the pressures of upholding family traditions at the chateau were lessened.

After the dishes had been put away, she curled up in a window seat and tried for awhile to read from an old history of the area she had discovered in one of the bookcases, but her eyes kept straying out to the cows grazing under the walnut trees and to the yellow poplars shimmering in the sun which had just come out.

Finally she laid the book aside, and emptying the walnuts from one of the baskets into a burlap bag she found in a cupboard, went outside to gather for the evening meal some of the swollen fruit from a fig tree by the kitchen door.

A pearl gray cat with half a dozen kittens trailing after it soon came to wind its tail about her legs. Setting the fruitfilled basket aside, she settled herself on the kitchen steps and watched with serene amusement the kittens pouncing on the fig leaf she dragged along through the dirt before them.

Half an hour later Philippe discovered her there.

"Did you have a pleasant sleep?" she inquired lazily, feeling herself as relaxed as the kitten stretched in her lap.

He sat down beside her. "I feel I could take on the world. What would you like to do?"

She leaned back on her elbows. "Nothing in particular. Except—" She set her head to one side. "I noticed a little punt down by the river this morning. Could we have a ride in it?"

"I'd like that. How good are you with a pole?"

She smiled up at him. "Fishing, or otherwise?"

He laughed. "Propelling the boat is what I had in mind, but since you've mentioned it, why shouldn't we try our hand at pulling a few fish out of the water? Trout amandine for dinner? How would you like that?"

"With you as the cook? I'd love it!"

In all, they hooked four fine fish, which Philippe, under the watchful eyes of the cat and her kittens, cleaned by the back door just before fresh showers began. Humming, he set about cooking them while Britt had a bath and changed into a long green dressing gown that matched her eyes and looked, she assured herself after careful scrutiny in the mirror, enough like a lounge dress to avoid suggestiveness. Not for the world would she want Philippe to think that anything about her tonight was intentionally seductive.

However, when she started down the stairs, he was emerging from the kitchen and from the sensuous manner in which his eyes moved over her, she knew despite her care, she had failed.

She halted, her hand on the railing. "I was just coming down to look for a match before I dress," she said quickly. "It's rather chilly upstairs, and I thought I'd get a fire going."

"No need to change." His gaze settled on the open collar of the gown. "We're in the country, after all and not expecting anyone. Besides, if you come along just as you are, we'll have enough time for a drink before dinner's ready."

Reluctantly she came down the rest of the way, apprehension chilling the pleasant warmth left over from the day's activities. But Philippe seemed not to notice her hesitation and when she had seated herself at one end of the sofa, instead of sitting down beside her, he took a chair at the opposite end of the fire.

"I had a lovely day," she said quietly when he had handed her a drink and settled himself with one of his own.

He stared into the flames. "I imagine," he answered in a tone matching hers, "that's your subtle way of telling me you hope the evening goes as well."

She swallowed. "I'm sure it will."

He gave her a keen-eyed glance and took a sip of his drink. "I enjoyed the day, too," he said in a lighter vein. "You're a fine companion."

Her cheeks warmed. "If a bit cruel at times," she murmured. "Am I forgiven?"

A muscle rippled across his jaw. "If I say yes, it doesn't mean I want you any less."

"I can't do anything about that."

When he said nothing, she went on. "I realize now that some of my earlier responses to you were misleading." She stared down at the glass in her hand. "I gave you the wrong impression and you decided to bring me here. Then I disappointed you. Or perhaps disgusted you is a better way of saying it. But in spite of all that, Philippe, and in spite of the clumsy way I handled things last night, you've shown me a pleasant time." She lifted eyes bright with tears. "You've shared your haunts with me and made me feel—" She shook her head helplessly. "—cherished."

"Because that's what you are." His voice throbbed with controlled emotion. "Cherished." The word on his lips took on a magical quality that set her heart racing.

"You're quite a woman," he went on in the same hoarse tone. "Not the saucy little girl I first imagined you to be."

"You were attracted to that girl," Britt said in a small voice.

"Like a moth to a flame," he agreed. "I expected to get singed." His dark eyes glowed in the firelight. "But the burn turned out to be fatal."

A smart reply that might have lightened the moment eluded Britt, and the tenderness she felt she dared not voice.

"Last night," he went on, "I thought all manner of

horrible things about you. Then this morning when I watched you setting our lives in order for the day, making do with this sullen, brutish lout you were trapped with in the country—"

"Don't, Philippe—!"

"The pieces began to fall in place," he continued, undeterred by her objection. "I began to recognize you, Britt Ryan, for the person you are." He set down his glass. "Are you ready for this?"

She stopped breathing.

"I think I'm in love with you."

Her lips parted.

"Love," he repeated softly. "That's the name of your game, isn't it?"

She found her voice. "I play for keeps," she whispered.

He gave a low laugh. "Don't I know it!"

He covered the space between them and took her in his arms. For one terrible moment she wondered at his sincerity. Was this just another ploy? If he said he loved her, did he think then she would come willingly to him?

But in another instant, all doubts vanished in recognition of the new way he held her. There was tautness still in his lean lines, and searching in the warm firmness of his lips, but the feverish urgency of last night's embrace was missing.

The man who held her now had made time in his heart for the slow ripening of love based on understanding, on caring. . . .

He cherished her.

Britt's heart sang, and she nestled joyfully into his arms.

Suddenly the door of the *séjour* burst open, admitting a blast of cold air mixed with rain and wind. A harsh voice rang out in the room. "How very cozy!"

Britt and Philippe sprang apart.

"Margo!" Philippe glared. "Didn't anyone ever mention that it's rude not to knock?"

The blond girl swept into the room, her tawny eyes ablaze. "This is the home of my fiancé. All doors should be open to me."

"And obviously you think they should stay open," he muttered, brushing past her to close out the wind and the rain.

Margo turned her blazing eyes on Britt. "What a slimy trick! Waiting until I left, then sneaking off up here with Philippe."

"No slimier," Philippe said drily, "than hiring spies. There was more than one, wasn't there?"

She flashed an angry look at him. "From appearances here, I should have hired an army." She turned again to Britt. "I warned you, you stupid fool. Too bad you didn't have the sense to listen to me as you pretended."

"I wasn't pretending. That was your idea."

"Take off your coat," Philippe commanded Margo. "There's a great deal we need to talk about."

She plopped herself by the fire and threw her damp wrap on a chair. "On that much at least we can agree."

"But any discussion will have to wait until after dinner," he said calmly. "I've trout amandine ready for the table, so dismiss your driver or whoever brought you out here and let's sit down to it."

"I drove myself," she replied haughtily.

All the better, thought Britt. The prospect of sharing dinner with Margo was dreadful enough without having to consider that she might be spending the night as well.

The meal went smoothly. Anger, it seemed, served as a stimulant to Margo's appetite. While Britt only picked at her fish, Margo had two servings and was even gracious enough to compliment the chef as they left the table.

"I shall miss those impromptu Sunday night suppers you used to fix for us on cook's night off," she said to Philippe when they had gone again to sit in the *séjour*.

Britt's heart leaped, and she cast a swift glance at Philippe who seemed as surprised as she at Margo's use of the past tense. Was she giving up then, without a fight?

"And you," said Margo leveling a hard look at Philippe, "will miss the chateau, no doubt."

He uncoiled like a spring from the sofa. "Miss it? What are you talking about?"

"Our future, Philippe." She turned a cold gaze on Britt. "Or are we to have separate futures now that she's come into the picture?"

Before he could reply, she said, "Are you going to marry me or not?"

Her bluntness threw Philippe. To Britt, time seemed to stop while he searched for an answer. "That's one of the things we must discuss," he said finally.

A smile more like a sneer lifted Margo's lips. "Then you haven't really decided, have you, whether or not your little Cornish fishergirl is worth throwing me over for?" Her scornful gaze swept Britt. "Surprised?" she said archly.

In truth, Britt *was* surprised. Shocked, actually. The moments after Philippe had declared himself to be in love with her had been too brief for any talk of marriage, but Britt realized now that subconsciously she had translated his words into a proposal. But Philippe had hesitated too long over Margo's question to have reached the same conclusion himself. The nucleus of joy that had sustained her through the strained meal hardened now into a lump of fear in the pit of her stomach. She was the outsider here, not Margo, and she wished with all her heart she were anywhere else in the world.

"What did you mean about the chateau?" Philippe persisted.

Margo found a cigarette in her expensive handbag, and waited while Philippe lifted a candle flame to its tip. Through the whirling smoke she exhaled she sent him a heavy-lidded stare. "Whether you continue to own it or not is your choice entirely."

"There's no question of that," he snapped.

Her lips curved upward. "Would you cling to it at the cost of the family name?"

"What kind of nonsense is this?" he exclaimed.

"It's a bargain, Philippe."

"Then state your terms," he said loftily, his eyes cold.

"These are your choices. Either you announce our engagement at the masquerade ball as planned and marry me in December, or you deed me the chateau."

Philippe's face relaxed. "Choices!" He laughed. "Your side is rather heavily favored, I'd say."

Her gaze hardened. "Not when you consider the other alternative."

"What might that be?" he said with a smile.

"If you refuse to marry me or to deed me the chateau, I'm prepared to go to the Paris press with a story about you that will knock their ears off."

Britt spoke for the first time. "Do you mean *La Revue?*" She almost laughed. "Do you think they'd care what you said about Philippe and me? I'm not even employed there!"

Margo's malicious laughter sounded discordant in the cozy *séjour.* "That doesn't surprise me at all. I never believed your ridiculous pretense of photographing and interviewing. You came to Chateau de Laon to snare Philippe Dolman, and when you failed there, you transferred your shabby little tryst to the countryside. But it isn't going to work here either." Her tawny eyes flicked back to Philippe. "Unless you're fool enough to want it to."

"I've never sought the social spotlight as you have, Margo." Philippe's contemptuous tone came as a shock to Britt. Even in their worst disagreements, he had never spoken in such a way to her. "The Paris column or scandal sheets, or whatever you have in mind, can say what they want of me. I couldn't care less."

Margo's eyes narrowed. "Philippe." Her voice held a deadly note. "I am not speaking of common ordinary bedroom antics. I'm talking about decadence."

He frowned. *"Decadence?"*

The blond girl crushed out her cigarette and rose. "Let me make this quite plain. I intend to live the rest of my life in the Chateau de Laon." Her gaze bored into the perplexity filling Philippe's dark eyes. "I can live there with you, Philippe. Or without you. But make no mistake about this: I have the weapon to make the chateau mine, and if you force me to, I'll use it."

Philippe recovered himself as she reached the door. "You're still the silly schoolgirl you were at fifteen," he scoffed. "The queen of the dramatics society. When you're able to carry on a mature conversation, I'll expect to hear from you."

"Oh, you'll hear." Margo's voice was low and throaty and pregnant with vague threats so ominous that a shiver of dread rippled up Britt's spine. "I'll be in Tours until the end of the week. Where I go from there depends on whether you come to fetch me home." She opened the door. "Or whether my lawyer comes to fetch you to court."

"Philippe?" Britt's voice broke the silence that had

shrouded them ever since the door closed behind Margo. "What is she going to do?"

"Nothing probably. She's bluffing. Blackmail is second nature to spoiled, selfish people like her. She's had her way about everything all her life. The possibility that we might not marry is something she can't handle any other way than with empty threats and histrionics."

Britt stared at him. The *possibility* that they might not marry. She clung to the back of a chair. "She cares a great deal for you," she heard herself say.

"She doesn't care a pin for me!" Philippe snorted. "Nor I for her. Whatever else there is between us, caring isn't part of it."

"And yet you're still considering marriage to her."

He crossed swiftly and took her in his arms. "I know this is difficult for you to understand, darling. Arranged marriages, marriages for convenience or property or to maintain bloodlines aren't a part of your background."

That brief statement delivered with such assurance did more to crystallize Britt's feeling of being an outsider than all of Margo's venomous outpourings. She stiffened. "You're quite right, of course."

Immediately he sensed her coolness. "Such things are as foreign to you as your idea of love as a foundation for marriage was to me."

He tightened his hold on her. "I never expected to care deeply for any woman, Britt. I never pictured myself as a man enslaved by any emotion and certainly not by love."

Abruptly he released her and jamming his hands into his pockets, turned toward the fire. "Above all else, I've treasured my right to come and go as I please, to set the tempo of my life as I alone saw fit."

"Do you think love will preclude those things?" she said softly.

He turned back to her. "It already has."

She stared at him. "And you don't like it?"

His chin jutted stubbornly. "No."

Now it was she who turned away. "I see." She took a wavering breath. "Then you've no problem, have you? If you go ahead with your plans to marry Margo, you won't sacrifice anything that's important to you."

"She's threatened me!" he exclaimed angrily. "I could never give in to that."

Britt felt an enormous weight pressing down upon her, compacting her into some minuscule version of herself she'd never recognize again. Philippe was rejecting her and seemed not even aware of doing so. The precious moment of confession which Margo had interrupted would never come again, and the stony truth of that was unbearable.

"I'm tired," she said without looking at him. "I'm going up to bed."

"Yes, go on," he said indifferently. "Where did I lay my slicker, do you know? I need a walk in the fresh air."

"I hung it in the cupboard by the back door," she replied.

"Good night then."

Chapter 15

When Britt came down the next morning after a long night of fitful sleep, she found the dinner dishes still on the table in the dining room, Margo's crushed out cigarette emitting a foul smell from the ashtray in the *séjour*, and Philippe sound asleep in his clothes on the sofa.

Fearful that she might wake him, she let her eyes touch only briefly the thick lashes that swept his cheek, the stubborn chin, the full, sensuous mouth, just the sight of which was enough to set her trembling.

Shutting the door softly, she went about tidying up the kitchen clutter and the dishes she had brought in with her. She had lived here almost as a wife, she reflected. Cooking, cleaning, gathering produce from the farm. A farm wife. She leaned against the wooden drainboard and closed her eyes. What if Philippe had been a farmer instead of a prominent landowner whose family dated back hundreds of years? What if instead of the chateau, he had owned only this walnut orchard, the white cows grazing in the meadow, the gray cat and her kittens?

Tears trickled down her cheeks. *I would have*

churned in this kitchen, she though sadly, *and fed my babies here, all of whom would have had strong chins and long black lashes that swept their cheeks when they slept.*

"Britt—"

She whirled, dabbing hastily at her damp face. "Philippe. Did I wake you?"

Still half asleep, he stared at her, his hair tousled, his eyes heavy-lidded. Longing so fierce it all but made her cry out racked her. She would never sleep beside him, never wake in the morning to kiss his mouth, curving now in a drowsy smile.

He crossed and put his arms around her, his hand pressing her head against his chest. "You're so industrious," he murmured. "Up at the crack of dawn, off to do the milking."

His lightheartedness was more painful than anger would have been, she was ashamed to realize. It meant that the yearning and anguish she had battled with through the long night were not shared by him. The sweetness that had passed between them was already forgotten.

But in a moment she knew how wrong she was.

As if he had taken her into his arms only to lead her back with him into the dream world from which he had come, he moved his lips on hers. Their searching into the warm softness of her own mouth spoke to her in a language that needed no words of reassurance. The hands that slid down her hips, then up across her back were reaffirming that she was his. They took the shape and measure of her in a way that said far more of what she meant to him than syllables and sentences ever could have done.

The embrace shook her as nothing had since she had come to love him. The passion in his kiss, so controlled, yet so promise-filled made contact with the deepest core of her being. What they were sharing now, she realized dizzily, made a mockery of the torrid conflicts that had torn them apart before. This was truth. This was love.

After a time he released her slowly and led her to a sunny corner of the kitchen.

"I spent half the night thinking," he said when they were seated beside each other, her hand in his, their eyes still filled with the magic of the world that had just opened before them. "I'm going to Tours this morning."

Britt reeled from the impact of his words.

But before she could speak, he went on. "I think you were right to be worried about Margo's threat. Whatever she has in mind to do—providing I refuse to heel to her—is sinister. I'm so accustomed to her dramatics I couldn't see that last night, but you sensed it, and I have to find out what it is."

Britt had lost her bearings completely. In his arms she had known with complete assurance that he was hers alone, and within a minute he had shattered her strongest confidence. He was going to Margo. Was there any place in the world she herself could go to escape the desolation suffocating her now?

As if reading her mind, he said, "I want you to stay here—if you think you can, all alone, and wait for me."

Britt tried to comprehend what he was saying. Wait for him? "What for?" she said woodenly.

"Because you're a part of me now," he said. "Just now—didn't you feel it? Didn't you know it?"

She caught her breath sharply. "Yes! Oh, yes—yes!"

He smiled. "Then you know nothing in the world can separate us."

She couldn't stop herself. "Then why go to Margo? Stay with me, Philippe! Can't we forget we ever knew Margo?"

"She's too entangled in my life to do that," he said gently. "I'm her guardian. She's lived in my home for years, I've handled her estate, advised her financially—"

"Of course. I understand," Britt murmured. "But oh, I wish—!"

"So do I, darling." He brought her hands to his lips. "But this is a problem we have to work out. I have to find out what she plans to do and then convince her that no matter what it is, she can't win. She and I will never be married."

Britt felt as if the sun had suddenly risen inside her. "You're not going to marry her? You're certain?"

He laughed. "Of course. Didn't you know that last night?"

Britt blinked. "You thought I knew?"

He gave her a puzzled smile. "I'd already told you I loved you before Margo came. Did you think I didn't mean that?"

"But you acted so strangely after she was gone. So—indifferent to me. When I said you could go on with your plans to marry Margo, you didn't deny that you were going to. The only thing you seemed upset about was that she had threatened you."

He signed. "I did object to that. Strenuously. I still do. I can't imagine what possessed her."

Britt paled. "I gave that some thought myself after I went to bed. I think it may be my fault."

"Yours? Why do you say that?"

"I let her think— Well, she was so certain she could keep us apart that I pretended things had gone much farther between us than they actually had. When she found me here—" Britt's voice died under her embarrassment.

Philippe grinned wickedly. "Ah! So you've gotten a

little of your own back! That must have caused an uncomfortable moment or two."

"More like half the night," she murmured.

He leaned across and kissed her lightly. "Don't worry, darling. I think there's more to Margo's motives than you could have stirred up, and whatever it is I intend to get to the bottom of it today, but as far as marriage to her is concerned—" He shook his head. "Never."

Britt appeared reassured, but one uncertainty still troubled her. "There was another reason for me to think you might go ahead with your plans," she said. "You dislike the changes loving me has brought into your life." She recalled the strong jutting of his chin, the irritation in his eyes when he had stood, hands jammed into his pockets, before the fire. "You were quite plain about that."

He reddened slightly. "It's true that I sometimes feel a bit shackled." He grinned ruefully. "But if I tried to hide that, soon enough those bright eyes of yours would ferret it out, so I might as well confess it, hadn't I?"

The color drained from her face. "Then how can we be happy together?"

He leaned across and kissed her tenderly. "Because, my darling," he said in a teasing tone, "I'll grow accustomed to the leg irons and the ball and chain. After a while I'll forget entirely the joys of the unshared life. In fact, one or two aspects of prison life I'm already beginning to appreciate." With one finger, he lifted her chin. "Waking up this morning, for example, and finding you here."

He kissed her again. "I want always to find you here—or wherever I am." He traced the soft curve of her cheek. "If I chafe a bit from time to time," he murmured, "you won't mind too much, will you?"

"Not if I'm certain you're happy," she whispered.

He gathered her into his arms then, and once more she lost herself in the wonder of his closeness.

"Certain?" he said at last.

She sighed deeply. "Certain."

Chapter 16

As soon as he had disclosed to Britt his plans to go to Tours to see Margo, Philippe telephoned the chateau, and shortly after lunch one of the estate men arrived, driving the Ferrari.

"I'll drop him off in Limoges," said Philippe as he bade goodbye to Britt. "The stableboys are bringing the horses up from the chateau today in preparation for the meet, and he can keep them company. He'll be glad for a holiday," he added with a grin. "Back at the chateau he'd be cutting grain."

From the front door of the farmhouse, Britt watched the Ferrari speeding away and recalled with a pang the day Philippe had driven her so recklessly to the chateau. That seemed a million years ago, so much had happened in between.

. What would happen now? she wondered, sitting down on the front steps. What would Margo tell

Philippe when he confronted her with the news that no matter what she did, they would not marry?

Clouds suddenly covered the sun and a chill breeze came up out of the east. Britt snuggled more closely into her sweater. Rain again today probably. Despite what she had told Philippe about being perfectly content to stay here alone, there was a difference, she was discovering, between enjoying a solitary walk or a book by the fire when another person was somewhere in the house, and finding contentment when no one else was there at all. Philippe had hardly been gone five minutes, and already she was feeling depressed.

Well, she wouldn't allow it!

She stood quickly. There were walnuts which needed to be spread for drying on the wire trays Philippe had showed her in one of the outbuildings, and mushrooms to gather, and more nuts, too, if the rain held off.

She could write a letter to Sydney and walk into the village to mail it. There were fruit jars in the cupboard; she could boil up a pot of figs and bottle them. The hours would pass, she assured herself, and Philippe would return.

Besides, there were dozens of happy thoughts she could occupy her mind with. Philippe loved her! That was some kind of miracle in itself and one she'd not had half enough time to consider.

Humming, she went back into the house, choosing the writing of a letter to Sydney as her first duty. The walk into the village and back occupied most of the rest of the afternoon. At five she made herself a pot of tea, stirred up the fire in the *séjour* and settled down once again with her history book.

At a quarter after the hour, she heard a car coming up the lane. Looking out the front window, she could hardly believe her eyes. The Ferrari was coming over the cattle crossing.

"What happened?" she cried when Philippe swung open the door and stepped out. "You couldn't have been to Tours and back in this short time."

"I only had to go as far as Limoges," he answered curtly, and her heart turned over at the grimness of his expression.

"Come inside then," she said as calmly as she could. "I've made a pot of tea."

But once in the *séjour* Philippe went straight to the liquor cabinet and poured himself a generous measure of Scotch.

"It's something terrible, isn't it?" said Britt when he had come to sit beside her.

"It's out of all reason," he answered numbly.

"Tell me!"

"Margo is prepared to take me into court on a morals charge."

"What?"

"She plans to claim I violated my position as her legal guardian."

Britt frowned. "I don't understand. Do you mean she thinks you've mishandled her finances?"

"She's going to claim I've mishandled *her*."

Britt's jaw dropped.

"She's going to say," he went on tonelessly, "that I went to her bedroom and attempted to seduce her."

"Philippe!"

He snorted in disgust. "Did you ever hear such trash?" Setting down his glass sharply, he strode to the fire. "And won't the scandal sheets love that! I could cheerfully wring her lily-white neck."

Britt stared, dumbfounded. "How did you learn this?"

"She was there. In Limoges. On the way back yesterday she met the Rimbauds, friends of ours. They have horses coming up for the meet too and decided to check on them, so Margo joined them instead of going on to Tours. When I stopped at the stables to let out Raoul, there they all were."

"So you had your talk in Limoges." Britt tried to sort her jumbled thoughts. "She told you there of this horrible plan?"

He nodded. "We keep rooms in Limoges during the meets. All the riders do. We went into one of those."

Britt's eyes opened wide. "This is where you are supposed to have assaulted her?"

"Oh, no, no. She figured all this out some time ago. The supposed seduction," he said with bitter sarcasm, "took place at the chateau."

"How ridiculous!" cried Britt. "Especially since you and Martinique go to such pains to see that Margo is properly chaperoned. Of course," she admitted, "if either of you had wanted to carry on an affair, you could easily have managed it, but as far as propriety is concerned, your reputation is entirely safeguarded, it seems to me, by the presence of Martinique. The court would uphold those arrangements, wouldn't it?"

"I'm sure it would." He sighed. "But there's a hitch. The night Margo came back from Nice, Martinique wasn't there. Margo was supposed to stay at least a week in Nice. Martinique was still at her cottage."

Britt's spirits sank. "Naturally that would be the night Margo would single out."

"I'm afraid so."

Suddenly Britt's eyes shone with new hope. "But I was at the chateau that night."

"Yes, but isolated in the south wing." He smiled glumly. "There's no way you could have known what went on in the other part of the house."

Britt was silent for a moment. Then she spoke in a

clear voice. "I'll say then that you spent the night with me. I'll testify that you were never out of my bedroom the entire evening."

Philippe regarded her with amazement. "You realize what that implies?"

"It's certainly a more acceptable situation, isn't it, than—" Margo's descriptive noun came to mind. "Than decadence."

"One hell of a lot more acceptable." He slumped again on the sofa. "No one would be much concerned over—what did Margo call it?—'bedroom antics'— between the two of us, but between a guardian and his ward—particularly if the ward is unwilling, as she'll of course claim—that's quite another matter."

"Then it's settled," said Britt shakily. "We needn't worry any more about it."

He eyed her keenly. "What you would claim, Britt, isn't true."

"Neither is Margo's claim!"

"Yours is just as farfetched," he answered quietly.

"No one need know that but you and I."

He looked at her for a long moment. "You'd publicly testify to have done what you never would have in order to save my name?"

She raised her green eyes. "Wouldn't you do it for me?"

Swiftly he pulled her to him and buried his face in her hair. "Is this part of love too?" he said hoarsely. "Sacrifice?"

"Every detail of our lives now is a part of love." Her muffled answer came from his chest where she had laid her head to hear his heart beat, its steady rhythm calming her agitation. "We're too strong for Margo, Philippe. There's no way she can hurt us."

But she felt his tenseness. "I'm afraid there is. She has witnesses."

Britt sprang back. "What are you saying?"

"I did go to her room that night."

Britt could scarcely breathe. "You were with her?"

"No, of course I wasn't 'with her.' At least not in the sense she's claiming, but I can't deny I was there, and her spies will testify to that."

His glance took in Britt's ashen face. "Oh, darling," he said quickly. "Don't look as if the world has come to an end. We'll figure our way out of this somehow."

Britt spoke without inflection. "What were you doing in her room?"

"Oh. That's what's worrying you, is it?" His jaw hardened. "Isn't trust one of love's virtues as well as sacrifice?"

"Don't be cruel!"

At once he was contrite and brought her to him again. "I'm sorry, darling. It's just that this is such a damnable mess. It's made me bitter."

Britt said nothing.

"But that doesn't answer your question, does it?" He sighed. "I'm hedging because the answer is so incredible. Margo's ruse to get me to her room was so obviously a setup I should have known at once she was up to something. But that it might be *this*—why, it simply never occurred to me!"

He took Britt's hand. "You see, that night after you went up to bed, Margo and I sat for awhile in the study. There were some details about the ball she wanted to discuss, and we had a nightcap. Then just as she was leaving to go to bed herself she mentioned casually that she had some suggestions for remodeling her apartment into one we could occupy after our marriage.

"As you perhaps know, the purpose of my redecorating the east wing was so that we could occupy that, but I wasn't ready to disclose that. And I especially wanted to avoid a discussion of it that particular night—" He squeezed Britt's hand. "Because by that time I was having serious second thoughts about the marriage itself. So when she insisted that I see what she had in mind, I gave in. She said to give her a few minutes while she had some furniture switched around in the apartment."

As Philippe continued to speak, Britt felt the anguish which had gripped her lessening its hold. Margo had tricked him into coming to her bedroom. He hadn't gone there voluntarily. As long as that were true, she could handle whatever else he had to tell her.

"She rang for a couple of the servants to tend to the furniture," Philippe went on, "and she said she'd send one of them to tell me when she was ready for me to come."

Britt sighed. "Oh, Philippe. And she called *me* naïve."

He flushed. "I know. I tell you, it never occurred to me to be suspicious. I thought it was just another of Margo's selfish unreasonable ideas."

"She'd count on your thinking that."

"She counted on something else too. She made me wait an hour. It was late. Finally I decided she'd given the whole thing up, and I changed into my night clothes. I was half asleep when a maid came and knocked on the door."

"To tell you her mistress was ready for you." Britt shook her head sadly. "The same maid you fired, of course?"

He nodded. "And there was another one I met in the hall on my way to Margo's apartment."

"But they don't know what went on once you were inside," Britt said in a more hopeful tone. "How can they attest to that?"

"Margo screamed."

"*Screamed?*"

His jaw tightened. "When I came in, she was up on a little table holding up a piece of drapery. Instantly she seemed to lose her balance. I broke her fall, but not before she shrieked. She made quite a noisy thing of it."

Britt sank back on the couch. "Dear heaven."

"Incredible, isn't it. I'm amazed she had enough time to think out all the details on as short a flight as the one from Nice."

Britt looked thoughtful. "Perhaps she didn't. I'm more inclined to think she plotted all this sometime ago and was keeping it ready for a rainy day."

"What do you mean? Why would she have?"

"She was quite emphatic when she told us she planned to live the rest of her life in the chateau."

"Living there is an important element of her social prestige. It's the main reason she wanted to marry me, I'm sure."

"This scheme was her insurance then, in the event you didn't propose."

"You're saying, in other words, that she'll have the chateau at any cost."

"She said so herself."

For a while they were quiet, each one lost in his own thoughts. Finally Britt said, "What are you going to do?"

"The only thing I can. Talk her out of it."

"Do you think you'll be able to?"

"I couldn't today, but I plan to have another go at it."

"You're going to Tours after all?"

"No. She'll be in Limoges with the Rimbauds for two more days. I'll go back to see her in the morning."

Britt's heart sank. It seemed to her, looking at Philippe's weary countenance, that part of Margo's plan might be to wear him down to the point where he would finally give in. Certainly each time she could force him to come to her put him in the position of beggar and strengthened her own stand.

"What if you just ignored her threats?" Britt offered tentatively.

Philippe shot her a surprised look. "Let her take me to court, do you mean?"

"Do you really think she'll go that far?"

He flushed angrily. "Of course she will. Not five minutes ago you said as much yourself."

"No," she said slowly as if she were seeing their plight for the first time. "I was quoting Margo when I said she'd have the chateau at any cost. But now that I've had a few minutes to think about it, I doubt that she's reckoned the cost."

"You're talking nonsense."

His curtness hurt, but she tried to keep in mind how much was at stake and went on patiently. "You see, Philippe, if she does drag you into court, no matter how the case turns out she will have injured herself."

"How?"

"If you're proven guilty—" she swallowed. "You won't be, of course, but if you were, there would always be people in Margo's social set—just as there are in every stratum of society—willing to believe the worst. They'd always wonder and discuss whether or not she'd enticed you. On the other hand, if you were acquitted, then she'd certainly look like a fool."

Philippe's chin came out. "What difference would any of that make?" he said crossly. "It would all be after the fact by that time. Your argument works both ways, you know. Whether I win or lose, doubts will have been planted in the minds of those who now regard me highly."

Are you including me as one of those? Britt wondered uneasily. *Or does my opinion no longer count?*

"Please listen to me with an open mind, Philippe. What I'm saying is that Margo will never carry things that far. She's a clever girl. Let her stew in her own juice for a time, and she's bound to realize that the nastiness she's threatening you with will rub off on her if she drags it into the public eye."

Suddenly all hostility seemed to leave him. "You're a wonderful antidote for Margo's poison, do you know that? When I left Limoges I was ready to murder her." The strain eased from his face. "But she's not worth the effort, is she?"

An airiness took hold of Britt. "You'll find a way to handle her."

Coming to Britt, he lifted her chin tenderly and kissed her on the lips. "Of course I will. Don't worry."

Chapter 17

The evening passed swiftly. Britt made the chicken pie she'd promised and after dinner they took another walk by the river. The rain which had marred the earlier part of their stay was gone now, and the heavens shone with a million stars.

Gazing up at them, Britt said dreamily, "I can almost imagine the sky is the River Tet with its fairyland lights and that in a moment we'll come upon the hotel terrace in Perpignan."

Philippe brushed his lips against her cheek. "Do I sense in that remark a certain wistfulness?" he teased.

"In a way I wouldn't mind if we were back in Perpignan on the first evening we met," she admitted. "There are things I might have done differently."

"You wouldn't have fallen in love with me. Is that one?"

She nestled against him. "I'd never want to change that, no matter what happened."

"And anything could," he said with a return to his earlier grimness.

"Oh, now see what I've done. I've spoiled your mood."

But he moved on to another thought. "If we do manage somehow to come out of all this unscathed, what of your career, Britt?"

What career? she almost said. The photographs she had taken for Sydney and the material she had gathered for the article had passed so completely from her mind that she had difficulty now recognizing herself as the cocky girl who had bragged to Philippe in a grove of lemon trees that she might gain a place on the staff of *La Revue*. Now she said with complete conviction, "I never really wanted a career."

"I find that hard to believe."

"It's true nevertheless. I was only filling in my time working until—" She broke off, acutely embarrassed.

"Until Sydney asked you to marry him?" he probed gently.

"He could have asked a dozen times," she mumbled. "I'd never have answered yes."

He stopped and turned her to him. "What if I ask?" he said thickly.

Her heart came up in her throat. "Ask and see," she managed.

The moon shown on his face, the craggy wonderful face that long ago had won her heart. "When I solve my problems with Margo," he said huskily, "will you be my wife, Britt Ryan?"

"Oh, Philippe!"

He gathered her in his arms. The moonlight on the Dordogne, the stars in the sky, the luminescent moon . . . all paled beside the shining hope radiating from the two of them, assured that some day soon they would be one.

All morning Britt's heart sang. *Philippe had formally proposed. She had accepted.* There was no sweeter song than that. Even the loneliness which enveloped her as she watched the Ferrari disappear down the road to Limoges could not hold out long against the pure joy surging through her veins.

If she could have dissuaded Philippe from making the journey to Margo, she would have, but bringing it up again last night and spoiling their happiness was unthinkable, and this morning Philippe had been so optimistic, so certain he could change Margo's mind, that Britt hadn't the heart to discourage him.

Besides, how did she know he wasn't right in going again to talk to Margo? He knew her well—far better than Britt. His could be the right course after all.

For a time Britt walked in the orchard, gathering nuts, but mostly daydreaming. What would life be like in the Chateau de Laon? Far different, she was sure, when her role was that of mistress instead of guest. The prospect was so exciting she could scarcely calm herself enough to think sensibly about it, but of one thing she was certain. No wife who had ever occupied that magnificent dwelling had ever loved her husband more than she would love Philippe.

That was the fundamental thing. Everything else— her lack of proper training for such an awesome task as hostess of the grandest chateau in the land, her ignorance of the social world—all those details would take care of themselves somehow as long as first place in Philippe's heart belonged to her. She leaned against a thick tree trunk and closed her eyes. Dreams did come true—and on a much grander scale than one could ever imagine!

Toward noon when she was cutting a bouquet of dahlias from the front garden, singeing the woody stems as she went, she heard the familiar roar of the Ferrari, and in a moment it appeared at the end of the lane.

She was about to express her delight by shouting, "Welcome home!" but the words died in her throat when she saw Philippe's face— a carbon copy of the one with which he had returned yesterday.

"What happened?" A weird feeling of *déjà vu* took hold of her. This had all taken place before, and she hated it as much now as she had then, for it was plain all had not gone well in Limoges.

Tight-lipped, Philippe led her into the house. "She's agreed to listen at least," he said when they were seated before the cold grate.

"But that's wonderful!" Britt's eyes scanned his face. "Isn't it?"

"In one way."

"But you're not happy."

"You know Margo," he answered roughly. "She always has a price."

Something cold closed around Britt's heart. "What is it?"

"She won't discuss anything further until you've gone back to Paris."

Britt felt as if a brick had slammed into her face. Not so much because of Margo's ultimatum, but because it was so obvious Philippe had agreed to it. "Do you want me to do that?"

"You know I don't."

"But you accepted the provision nevertheless?"

The color in his cheeks deepened. "I'm negotiating with her, Britt!"

His obvious annoyance cut her, but she let the remark pass. "What did you say to her?"

"About her threat?" He seemed relieved to change the subject. "I told her I was sure she hadn't thought the matter through, that there would be repercussions I was certain she hadn't considered."

Britt waited.

"She was so agreeable it was amazing."

So graciousness was to be her tack, thought Britt, feeling all at once as if the earth were sliding from beneath her. No one could be more gracious than Margo when she put her mind to it.

Philippe went on. "She said perhaps she hadn't given the matter enough thought, and she'd be happy to hear what I had to say about it. But then when I started to tell her, she cut me off. 'Every minute Britt is at the farm,' she told me, 'complicates the case.'"

Britt forced a calmness into her voice. "I don't see how."

He frowned. "Think, Britt. If I'm forced to defend my morals, how will it appear if word gets out that I've had a girl here for a week?"

"A girl!" Her tone reflected the pain he had inflicted by his insensitive choice of words. "If that's all I am to you—some *girl*—"

He came at once and put his arms about her. "I'm only telling you how it will appear to others," he said soothingly, but his words seemed to bear an echo of Margo.

Britt's voice trembled. "Nothing we need be ashamed of has happened here, Philippe."

"*We* know that, but who else does?"

"I've never cared much about other people's opinions." Her green eyes shimmered. "That was one of the things you admired about me, as I remember."

His face took on a set look.

"Don't go back to see Margo," she pleaded. "Stay here. Let's be the way we are, Philippe, not the way she wants us to be."

"I can't risk that."

His words stung as nothing else had. "Not even for me?"

"Dammit, Britt! This is *all* for you."

She shook her head. "It's for the chateau."

"If I don't have the chateau," he said stonily, "I have nothing to offer."

"You have yourself!" She swallowed back her tears. "You're all I want."

He looked at her and suddenly his defensiveness melted. "I'm yours already," he muttered thickly, gathering her into his arms. "We're going to be married, remember? But first you must return to Paris. Just for a short time. I'll call you every day. Then when the whole mess is resolved, I'll come for you, and we can start our life together as we should, free of all entanglements."

He kissed her. "Can't you trust me to handle Margo, Britt? Isn't your love strong enough for that?"

Her tears spilled over. "Is yours?"

They clung to each other. His kisses covered her face, his powerful embrace closed out all but the assurance of his devotion. Finally he put her from him and said gently, "Go and pack your things now. I'll drive you to Limoges, and you can take the train from there."

Chapter 18

It was winter in Paris, if not according to the calendar, at least in Britt's heart. The gloom of the city streets contrasted dismally to the golden days along the Dordogne and even to the rainy ones, and depressed her in the same way the winter months had always done at Land's End. Ordinarily in Paris there was a gaiety which had a way of lifting her spirits at any time of the year, but in the dark days since she had ridden in on the train from Limoges, the lovely city had shown her only its coldest face.

Her rooms on the Rue de Mont had been invaded in her absence by an army of ants. Sydney's left leg had refused to mend properly, and he was back in traction. And despite Philippe's promise to call every day, a week had passed, and she had heard nothing.

She felt her deepest fears were now confirmed. She'd been right to believe that Margo would try to wear down Philippe's resistance. Perhaps by now she already had.

In a morning paper Britt had read, as best she could through her tears, the list of entrants in the equestrian meet. Both Margo and Philippe were named. Probably tonight the two of them and their friends, the Rimbauds, were enjoying dinner together. Laughing . . . talking. It was plain Philippe had forgotten her entirely. His proposal had been spawned in some vagary of his mercurial nature, and now back with his own kind, he had discarded it as easily as a ballast bag tossed from his balloon when it was no longer needed.

Sitting down at the small kitchen table in her flat, Britt stared absently at a trail of ants wending their way over the edge of a cabinet top. All her efforts to eradicate them had failed, but now she felt it no longer mattered if they took over the whole place. She had decided to move anyway, to carry out her plan to visit Aunt Tillie and then go up to London. This afternoon she had submitted to the editors of *La Revue* the photographs she had taken at the Chateau de Laon and the material she had gathered for the article. Her work in Paris was finished.

There was an irony to that too.

Since her return she had gone every day to the hospital, but this morning she had at last brought with her for Sydney's inspection the completed article and the photographs. When he had fumed previously at the delay she had begged him to be patient.

"The only way you can view them with the same perspective as the editors is by considering the photographs alongside the article. Then you'll be able to make criticisms, and I can make the necessary changes before we submit."

But according to the delighted Sydney, no changes were needed.

"My word!" he had cried. "They're super!" Twice more he ruffled through the glossy prints and referred to the paragraphs she had labored over for days. "What a gorgeous place, and you've captured it perfectly. It makes me want to get up, broken legs and all, and rush to see it. Can you imagine how the readers will react?"

"You think I can take it all over to your editor today then?" Britt's heart came up in her throat. "What will I say?"

"Make a clean breast of things," he had told her with amazing cheerfulness. "God knows how long I'll be laid up here. They're going to need somebody. It might as well be you."

"Do you really think they'll hire me?"

"Why not? You've done a smashing job." He had looked at her then with genuine concern. "It's not the job I'm worried about though. It's you. I've never seen you quite so—" He searched for the proper word. "Lifeless. I think the pace at the chateau might have been a bit rich for your blood."

She smiled wanly. "I guess it's a good thing I won't be subjected to it any further."

Dismal as her words were, they stirred hope in her. If her heart had mended enough for her to joke about her shattered plans for the future, then maybe her emotional state was not as desperate as she had feared.

That consolation, coupled with Sydney's praise had enabled her shortly after noon to present a brave face at the editor's desk where she made her explanations as succinctly as her dry mouth would allow.

"So you see," she concluded. "It was because of the stiff competition here at the magazine that Sydney preferred to keep his accident a secret and to submit my work in place of his. He felt if he couldn't come through with the chateau article he might lose his place here on staff."

The editor was highly annoyed. But not at Britt, as she had first thought. At Sydney for having concealed for so long his invalidism, a breach of friendship which the woman finally decided to forgive by ordering two dozen red roses and a five pound box of sweets to be delivered to his bedside.

Then she turned her attention back to Britt's photographs. While she perused them, Britt looked nervously about the office, a starkly modern space, too cold, in Britt's opinion, to be termed a room, but quite suitable for the brusque young woman behind the desk whom Britt could not imagine caring in the least for her photographs filled with the autumn light of coastal France and the mystery of the chateau's ancient shadows.

Finally the editor looked up and gave Britt a thorough scrutiny. "Sydney underestimates himself. There's competition at *La Revue,* yes, but when one is the best it doesn't matter." She looked over the rims of her heavy glasses. "And Sydney *is* the best." Her gaze bore into Britt. "You, however, are not far behind him. How would you like a job?"

That was the moment—the moment that had cost her so much to achieve—when Britt knew she was leaving Paris.

When the editor spoke the words she had so fervently wished to hear only a few weeks before, something in her snapped. She had come full circle, she realized numbly. When she had left Paris for Perpignan her goal had been to work on the staff at *La Revue.*

Now she had achieved it—and found it meaningless. It was time to move on.

Quickly she murmured her appreciation of the offer, collected payment for her work, and fled.

Back in her apartment she sipped absently from a cup of coffee grown cold. The sandwich she had made for her evening meal lay untouched on her plate, and she thought wryly what a feast it would be for the ants if she gave in to her strongest desire which at that moment was simply to get up and walk out of the apartment and never look back.

It would be symbolic of walking away from all that had happened to her in the days since she had come to know Philippe Dolman. He had proposed marriage, yes, but with a provision: *He had first to solve his problems with Margo.* She'd scarcely noticed his words at the time, so enthralled had she been in the wonder of his asking her to marry him. Now they haunted her. Obviously he had not been able to solve his problems with Margo. Even if he despised Margo, he would marry her before he would allow the slightest taint to his historical name or before he could face the prospect of giving up the chateau. She'd been a fool to think for even a moment that she might be more important to him than his heritage.

Still, nothing could ever make her forget the way she had felt in Philippe's arms or the way his mouth had moved on hers, speaking with a language only her heated passions could respond to. Even now just the thought of him, though he was miles away and in Margo's arms probably, made desire course through her veins like liquid fire.

Her heart twisted. If all she were to have out of life were memories, then what a fool she was not to have had the best.

She could have lain beside Philippe that night at the farm—and every night afterward. If she had done that—given in to all that was primitive and fundamental within her—he might even have resisted Margo's threats and stayed with her.

A sob escaped her throat. *To thine ownself be true.* Such a wise man, Shakespeare, but he ought to have defined what he meant by that phrase that had guided her the night she shoved Philippe away. Her baser nature was the self she should have listened to, not the puritan promptings which left her with a cold bed now and an even colder heart.

What did it matter to Philippe that she had maintained her integrity? Not enough certainly to have kept him true to her.

Loving Philippe had spoiled her for everything else too. Her life here in Paris. The job at *La Revue*. Everything that had once been bright and beautiful had lost its sparkle because of him.

Yet that wasn't quite true, was it? Or fair. Long before she had known Philippe, she had known restlessness, the longing she still had for husband, home, and children. The need to be cherished, as Philippe had vowed she was.

Oh, why must every thought bring her back to him! Was there no way she could find peace?

Suddenly she knew there was a way. She could go back to the farm. Peace was there beside the slumberous river, among the old walnut trees heavy with their bounty, in the simple hominess of the *séjour* where quiet gave way only to the ticking of an ancient clock on the mantle.

The farm was as close to home as any place Britt had ever known and with all her heart she longed to be there now. The beauty of it was there was nothing to stop her! Philippe would be in Limoges at the meet until Sunday. If she left tonight, she could have three whole days alone to say her goodbyes to everything that had won her heart by the Dordogne.

Trembling, she clasped her hands to her throat. That was most of what was wrong, wasn't it, now that she had faced the fact that Philippe was lost to her? The pain that remained still tortured her because Philippe had uprooted her so suddenly. She'd had no time to wean herself gently from what she had come to trust. She needed that time. And she would have it!

Obtaining the key to the sturdy old farmhouse was the only part of her adventure Britt dreaded, but when she arrived late the next afternoon in a hired car—a luxury she still couldn't believe she had treated herself to—Madame Londine was gathering hips and haws and spindleberries in a thicket near the gate and seemed overjoyed to see her.

"You've come back!" the ample lady cried. "And just at the right time too. I've cleaned the place from top to bottom and left it open to air. You can go right on, and later I'll send you up a bit of supper."

True to her word, Madame's young son arrived just before eight with a steaming pot of stewed chicken and vegetables and a loaf of crusty bread.

"*Fromage,* too," said the boy, producing a cheese in a string bag.

Britt took his offerings gratefully and gave him a bit of money for his trouble.

The boy went off whistling up the lane, and Britt bolted the door, carrying her delicious smelling treasure into the *séjour* where she had set up the little table on which she and Philippe had shared their meals.

The first few moments after she had entered the empty house, doubts had assailed her. This had been a foolish idea, a silly impulse she should never have responded to. Everywhere she found reminders of Philippe. A pipe on the desk, the pair of old boots he had worn into the orchard, their fishing poles tipped against one corner of the kitchen.

But gradually the warmth and coziness of the cottage

overcame her feeling of aloneness and she felt strangely enfolded again in Philippe's love.

She had done well to come back, she thought now, testing the tempting stew for hotness. This was the environment in which her wounds would heal. She would shore up her memories here and make them fast for the years to come. The house would give her courage; the grounds and the river, peace of mind. After she had gathered together her things in Paris she could go back to England, if not fulfilled, at least reconciled to a degree.

She ate with a hearty appetite and listened without alarm to the gradually rising wind which rattled the shutters and whistled about the chimney.

Chapter 19

Sometime toward midnight Britt woke to the increased howling of the wind and a heavy driving rain which struck the windowpanes of her attic room like a barrage of stones. Nestling further into the warmth of her bed she thought with gratitude of the barn safely sheltering the hired car. Thank goodness she had had the presence of mind before she came up to bed to go out and latch the door. Assured that everything, including herself, was safe and secure, she drifted peacefully back to sleep.

In the morning she woke to find the storm still raging, though with lessened intensity. Through the rain splattered window of the kitchen, she could see one big tree down in the orchard and the veritable rivers the garden paths had become.

Humming, she set about making her breakfast. The weather had cooperated perfectly with her plans to absorb all she could of the warm strength the house exuded. She could spend today curled up in the *séjour* reading and thinking and sorting out the pieces of her life which were still intact—much as one might if she were recuperating from a severe illness, she thought ruefully. In a storm like this she need fear no intrusions from the outside world. By tomorrow the disturbance would have all blown over and she could have her walk along the river and through the orchard.

The first part of the morning passed much as she had hoped. Madame Londine trudged over during a break in the rain, bringing a dozen eggs and a pail of fresh milk, but other than that interruption, Britt spent the hours in contented solitude.

She had just entered the kitchen to set about stirring up an omelette for lunch when over the sound of the dying wind she heard a familiar roar.

The Ferrari? Her heart stopped. It couldn't be!

Racing to the window, she took the corner of her apron and smeared steam from the pane. *It was!* And the little car had already passed over the cattle crossing.

She wheeled back toward the kitchen, panic-stricken. Philippe mustn't find her here. For a wild moment she thought of crawling into a cupboard. He was supposed to be in Limoges. Why wasn't he? Had something happened? Had he been injured at the meet?

Every other thought except his safety left her mind.

She rushed back to the window. There a totally unexpected sight greeted her.

Philippe was not alone.

Margo, dressed in a close-fitting riding habit, was emerging from the front seat of the car and just behind her, unfolding from the back, came a middle-aged couple who were strangers to Britt.

Paralyzed, she watched while Philippe paused near the bonnet of the car and pointed back toward the orchard. Margo said something, and the man and woman laughed. Then all four turned toward the — house.

One thought blazed across Britt's mind. Escape! She lunged toward the stair, but her foot had barely touched the second step when Philippe's puzzled voice came from the other side of the door.

"Why, it's not even locked."

Britt froze. The door swung open. Philippe's shocked gaze met her own.

"Britt? What on earth—!"

Faces crowding the doorway behind him blurred. She tried to speak and failed.

Philippe stepped forward, a stunned look on his face. "What are you doing here?"

"As if you didn't know!" Margo disengaged herself from the mass of accusing eyes trained on Britt and flung herself at Philippe. "What a lowdown, scheming, nasty trick."

"Certainly you don't think I knew she was here!" said the incredulous Philippe.

"Certainly I *do!*" Scarlet with rage, Margo faced Britt. "What happened?" she spat out. "Did you get your signals crossed and come creeping out of your hidey hole before you were supposed to?"

The bewildered couple in the doorway melted out

into the yard to the obvious relief of Philippe, who shut the door almost in their faces and then turned white-lipped to Britt.

"Explain yourself at once," he commanded.

His tone had the effect of a bucket of cold water thrown over her head. Britt's voice erupted harshly from her throat. "How decent of you to offer me the opportunity!"

"The charade is over." Margo glared at them both. "It's too late for explanations." Her lip curled. "Though I'm sure they'd be fascinating."

Philippe directed his anger at Margo. "Be quiet. Let's hear what she has to say."

Fury so intense it was suffocating swept over Britt. He could at least have granted her the dignity of her name! Planting her hands firmly on her slender hips, she spoke in a hostile tone that rang menacingly across the *séjour*. "I arrived last night. I was trapped by the storm. And I am now leaving."

As swiftly as a cat, Margo blocked her way. "Surely you can come up with a better story than that."

Philippe crowded up behind her. "Why did you return at all?"

The question knifed into Britt. "I left my camera here," she lied.

"Oh, *really*," said Margo.

Britt felt her face catch fire. "You can believe it or not. I couldn't care less."

Margo's eyes blazed. "I suppose next you'll say you flew out from Paris on a broomstick."

"I came in a hired car," said Britt through clenched teeth.

"Where is it?" demanded Philippe.

"In the barn." Tears stung Britt's eyelids. He had turned his back on her completely. "Madame Londine can easily verify the time of my arrival if the truth matters to anyone." Her voice broke. "Let me pass, please."

Margo remained where she was. "No suitcase?" she said coldly.

Britt caught her breath. The suitcase! And all her things strung about in the room upstairs as if she'd been here all the time. For an instant she thought she might faint, but one look at Philippe's closed face drove a fresh spurt of adrenalin through her bloodstream.

"I'll be back for it," she said coolly. "But first I'm going to invite your friends in. Since my presence here has caused a scene and embarrassed them, the least I can do is offer them a cup of coffee."

Her aplomb had a disquieting effect on Margo and on Philippe as well, and both stepped aside to let Britt pass. When she returned in a moment with the hesitant couple, Philippe had recovered himself enough to introduce them.

"Britt Ryan, may I present Elaine and Edouard Rimbaud. Miss Ryan has been at the chateau—" He cleared his throat. "And here at the farm photographing for her magazine, *La Revue*."

He went on in the face of Margo's saccharine smile. "I was under the impression she'd already left for Paris, so it was rather a surprise to find she'd not."

"We're quite pleased to meet you," Elaine Rimbaud said. It was clear from her expression she found Philippe's explanation a thin one, but she smiled graciously. "*La Revue* is a favorite publication of mine. Are you new on the staff? I don't seem to recall—"

"Quite new," Margo supplied in a dry tone. "There might even be one or two editors not yet aware she's been employed."

"Have a seat, Elaine," Philippe intervened quickly.

"You too, Edouard. I'll just step out in the kitchen and help Britt fetch the coffee—"

"I don't need any help," said Britt with unmistakable firmness. "I'll just be a moment."

But in the kitchen, she collapsed on a stool, trembling violently. Margo was despicable, but Philippe was worse! How could a man who had once professed love—proposed marriage even!—behave as he had done? Every word he had spoken was directed toward pushing her out of the house, she thought furiously, and how Margo was enjoying that!

Suddenly out of the blue a wild, crazy, wonderful idea popped into her mind. She got up swiftly and set the coffee pot on the stove. While it heated, she scurried about the kitchen like a madwoman, cracking eggs into a bowl . . . setting a tray with plates and silverware. . . .

When she finally sailed into the *séjour* with the coffee, her cheeks were rosy and her green eyes sparkled brightly. "Here we are. Wait until you hear what a smashing idea I've just had."

The Rimbauds looked up with anticipatory smiles, but Margo glared, and Philippe glowered darkly.

Britt gave one and all a dazzling smile. "We have just enough time for lunch together before I go."

"Lunch!" cried Margo.

Philippe came out of his chair. "Don't be absurd!" Then remembering his role: "What I mean is, the weather is so unstable. You mustn't delay getting on the road."

"I agree," said Margo barely disguising her anger. "Don't let us keep you."

"An hour more won't make any difference," said Britt airily. "I'm sure you're starving after your drive." She set the coffee tray down. "By the way, how is it that you've left the meet before its finish?"

"The weather, my dear," said Edouard Rimbaud, taking the cup she handed him. "The course is a muddy mess. In fact, the whole thing was canceled at dawn. It was still pouring when we left."

Britt made a clucking sound. "What a shame! But what a lucky break for me." She turned a brilliant smile on Margo. "It gives me a chance to have a nice visit with you. Now, if you'll excuse me, I'll just dash out and put the finishing touches on our lunch."

Philippe's voice knifed coldly across the room. "Don't bother, please. We had a late breakfast."

She shot him her sauciest smile. "No bother at all. The eggs are all ready for the omelette. The cheese is grated. The only problem is we haven't any fruit, but perhaps it won't matter if we have a sweet wine instead."

In less than a minute Philippe had followed her into the kitchen. "Just what is this all about?" he hissed. "Aren't things difficult enough without prolonging them?"

Britt pushed past him with her bowl of eggs. "Better not let dear Margo catch you fraternizing with the kitchen help."

He grabbed at her arm, but she eluded his reach. "You'll cause a spill!" she snapped. "Get out, please, and leave me alone."

He blocked her way to the stove. "Have you lost your mind? Jeopardizing everything that's important to us by antagonizing Margo?"

"Nothing that concerns you—or Margo—is important to me."

He paled. "Darling! You don't mean that."

"*Darling!* How dare you call me that?"

He caught her shoulders. "I love you, remember?"

"A fine way you have of showing it!"

"Things are very precarious, Britt!"

"Then don't make them more so. Wouldn't Margo love to walk in and find you touching me?"

His hands fell to his sides. "You're right, of course, but my God, I've missed you."

"Is that why you called every day?" she scoffed bitterly.

"I thought you'd understand. I don't know who she has spying on me. I couldn't risk it. But if I'd known you were here—"

"You'd have run a hundred miles in the other direction." Deftly she slid the eggs into the pan, anger sharpening her movements. "Fetch the wine, please," she said briskly just as Margo, hawk-eyed, appeared in the doorway with the coffee tray.

The lunch was a triumph for Britt, who, finding revenge a sweet appetizer, finished her portion of the omelette with glowing satisfaction. The Rimbauds, too, ate heartily, obviously convinced that the scene which had greeted them on their arrival concerned only some minor indiscretion and was of little significance.

But as Britt had hoped, Philippe and Margo were miserable. Margo's tawny eyes blazed as she picked at her food, unwilling as yet to reveal her hand in front of the Rimbauds, yet raging inwardly because Britt had outmaneuvered her.

Philippe chewed mechanically as he tried without success to keep up with Britt's bright chatter.

Finally, however, their ordeal was over. With the same sparkling smile Britt had worn throughout the meal, she pushed back her chair. "Now I really *must* run. I hope you'll forgive me, Margo, for leaving you with all the tidying up. I'm afraid the kitchen's a frightful mess, but as you suggested earlier, I really should be on my way."

In less time than it took the outraged Margo to carry

a plate to the kitchen, Britt was down again with her suitcase, saying her farewells.

"I'll carry your case to the car," said Philippe.

"I can manage nicely," Britt said, but Philippe ignored her.

When they rounded the corner of the house, he turned on her furiously. "You win the prize, do you know that? Subjecting us all to that grotesque meal."

"I thought it was rather tasty," she answered smugly. "Margo seemed to love it."

"You could wreck everything!"

Britt glared up at him. "I couldn't care less."

"If you don't care, then what are you doing back here?" he challenged.

She felt her face go hot and moved quickly ahead of him on the path. "I told you. I left my camera."

"I won't buy that," he said after her. "The last thing I handed up to you when I helped you on the train was your camera. *Sydney's* camera."

"Then I must have left it on the train," she mumbled.

He caught up with her at the barn door and turned her with a swift thrust of his hand. "Tell me the truth. Why did you come back?"

"I came to rob you!" she flung at him. "Be sure you check my suitcase before you put it in the car."

They glared at one another. All at once Philippe swept her to him. "What's happening to us?" he muttered thickly. "We have a precious five minutes alone, and we're wasting it quarreling."

Britt caught the scent of his skin, felt the warmth of it upon her face. Every instinct bade her yield to him, urged her to confess the love consuming her. For a moment she wavered. Then she pulled away. He was still playing the ends against the middle, and she'd had enough of that to last a lifetime.

In a toneless voice she said: "Are you going to open the barn door, or shall I do it myself?"

He stared at her. "Where are you going from here?"

"Does it matter?"

"Dammit, of course it does! Where can I reach you?"

"Why should you want to?"

He ignored that. "Back in Paris? Is the address the same?"

"No, it isn't, so don't waste your time. You won't be able to find me." She choked. "Not that you'd ever try."

He gripped her arms again. "Darling, I promise you it won't be long now. Have faith in me. Wait!"

"If there was ever anything to wait for, it doesn't matter now," she answered in a dead voice. "It's over, Philippe."

"Are you going back to Sydney? Is that it?"

A terrible weariness came over her. "What if I am? It's no business of yours." She lifted a blank face to his. "I don't want to hear your name or think of this place or the chateau ever again. Get out of my way, please."

She saw the pain spring into his dark eyes, and for an instant she came perilously close to relenting. How welcome had been the shelter of his arms . . . his face close against her own. . . . Then suddenly she remembered his accusing attitude and the way he had sided with Margo, bending over backward to assure her that he hadn't known that she, Britt, was at the farm.

Sickened, Britt turned away. Philippe hesitated only a moment longer. Then without a word, he swung open the barn door, and before she had turned the car around, he had vanished into the orchard.

Chapter 20

Britt spent the next four days after leaving the farm packing and preparing to leave Paris. A listlessness far worse than any she had experienced on her first return to the city possessed her. The slightest effort seemed to require all of her energy, and at the end of a day she felt as if she had spent its hours trudging through hip deep mud or pulling an ox cart.

Finally on the morning of the fifth day, she sent her bags ahead to the railroad station and stopped by the hospital to say goodbye to Sydney.

She found him in the midst of a frantic telephone conversation which he terminated immediately when he saw her in the doorway.

"Britt! Thank God! I thought I'd missed you."

She set down her train case. "I told you I wouldn't leave without stopping by. What's wrong?"

"Everything! The magazine called half a dozen times."

"*La Revue?* What does that have to do with me?"

"Everything," he said again as if it were the only word he knew. "You have to go back to the chateau."

"Chateau de Laon?" She gave a bitter laugh. "I wouldn't go there again for any reason ever."

"You must," he said decisively. "Today. They're flying you down."

"I'm on my way to Calais," she protested. "My ferry leaves at six this evening."

"At six this evening you'll be dressing for a costume ball." He picked up the telephone again. "Wait a second while I let my editor know I've found you at last."

Britt crossed quickly to his side. "Sydney! What is this all about?"

"I'll explain in a moment. The magazine is waiting to call Dolman."

"They mustn't do that!"

"Britt, my editor is beside herself."

"That has nothing to do with me."

"It has everything to do with you," he answered grimly. "Now sit down in that chair until I'm done with this," he commanded, "or I'll break your beautiful neck."

"You'll have to catch me first!" she answered indignantly.

"You walk out of here, and you'll take my job with you!"

Seeing the usually calm, affable Sydney in such a rage cowed Britt into doing as he ordered, and she listened numbly as he confirmed with his editor that Britt Ryan would be at the airport ready to go in an hour's time.

"There!" He replaced the receiver. "Thank God. If you hadn't shown up here, I don't know what I would have done."

"Well the first thing you have to do now is explain yourself," said Britt coldly, "and I'm *not* going to the Chateau de Laon no matter who thinks I am."

He stared solemnly at her. "You forgot the release, Britt."

She stared back blankly. "What release?"

"No publication can print an article or photographs of the type you submitted without the subject signing a release." His voice was fraught with strained patience. "I warned you about that, Britt. I even gave you the printed release form. Why didn't you follow through?"

Britt paled. "The release! I never once thought of it after—" She swallowed. "Philippe Dolman never mentioned it."

"He didn't have to. It was your responsibility. Worse than that," he went on, "Dolman claims he never saw the text of your article, never even saw the pictures. Good Lord, Britt! What were you thinking of down there? What were you doing?"

A wave of dizziness washing over her made the room spin. "He was so insistent at first," she began feebly. "He said he would want to check every word, supervise everything."

"He had a right to. It's his chateau. Naturally he'd want to know how it was to be presented."

"But then he forgot about it," Britt protested. "He didn't care about the article or the photographs. He never asked to see them."

Sydney gave her an incredulous look. "What in heaven's name did he think you were doing there then?"

"He— We— Oh, it's all too hopelessly complicated. Don't ask me to explain, please."

"The *magazine* is asking you, Britt! You have to produce some answers." Sydney sighed explosively. "Oh, hell. Let it go. Right now the issue is the masquerade ball. Get down there, do a bang-up job, and maybe they'll forget to draw and quarter you."

"What does the ball have to do with this?"

Sydney gave her a pitying look. "I don't know what's happened to you. You must have been hit by a bus or dropped on your head. Can't you see? The man wants retribution! He's got *La Revue* by the throat. He could sue the pants off us. But there's something big going on at the chateau tonight. This cockeyed ball. According to my editor, Dolman says it marks the most important occasion of his life, and he wants pictures, a story, the works."

Britt stared dumbly. *The most important occasion of Philippe's life: the announcement of his engagement to Margo. And he's seeing to it that I'm there to witness it.*

"I can't go, Sydney. They'll have to find someone else."

"He won't *accept* anyone else!" Sydney was all but shouting. "Aren't you listening to me? You're the one who bungled the original article. Now if this ball, the *finale,* isn't tacked onto it, *by you,* heaven knows what will happen. He's a powerful man. He could ruin the magazine."

Sydney lay back on the pillow and closed his eyes. "Why I ever let you talk me into this damned mess to begin with, I'll never know."

"You were happy enough when I showed you the photographs," said Britt, regaining a bit of her spirit.

"That was before I knew the sky was falling," moaned Sydney. He opened his eyes. "Britt, if you've a drop of compassion in your veins, get on that airplane. Get the pictures. If *La Revue* blackballs me, I'll never get another job anywhere."

Britt stared bleakly at him. "It's that important?"

"I can't *tell* you how important it is! Britt, please!"

The plane set down in the same meadow from which Philippe had launched the balloon the day he had taken Britt to the farm, except now instead of soft green, the grass was brown and frostbitten. Inside the chateau's formerly peaceful walls there was unbelievable activity.

The wide halls were filled with chattering guests and scurrying seamstresses darting in and out of apartments making last minute alterations of medieval costumes. The scents of expensive perfumes weighted the air, and everywhere a feverish excitement could be felt.

Britt, camera in hand, made her way slowly to the end of the south wing where the social secretary in the entry hall had directed her. She passed the elegant apartment she had formerly occupied and found, without surprise, that the room earmarked for her tonight was hardly larger than one of the closets in the other suite.

At the sounds of laughter mingled with conversation, she set the camera on a table and went to the window. Below, she saw Philippe was entertaining in the garden with a champagne party, and her heart thudded painfully as she watched him move with ease among his guests.

How traitorous the heart was, she thought. Here was a man who was vengeful and cruel, who had forced her to come here for the most painful ordeal of her life: witnessing his engagement to another woman. A man who had once professed to love her and whom—in spite of all this—she still loved.

How was that possible?

Yet, watching him, hearing his laughter floating up, she could not deny that this was so. Would she always love him? Years from now would the mere mention of his name strike a blow to her sensibilities? Would her pulse always race when she remembered the touch of his lips, his hands moving over her body?

She turned away from the window. How would she get through this night? How could she bear the sight of Margo, radiant in her victory?

A knock sounded at the door. Opening it, Britt met the smile of an excited maid. "Your costume, mademoiselle."

Britt stood aside as the girl entered, bearing a sleek velvet gown, the color of the sea. *The color of my eyes,* thought Britt, startled. "I'm sure there's a mistake," she said quickly. "I've brought my own costume."

Sydney had instructed her that a milkmaid's attire had been set aside for her at a costumery on her way to the airport, and it lay now in its box on the table beside her train case.

"You're Mademoiselle Ryan?" said the girl.

Britt nodded.

"This is correct then." The girl hung the dress, then laid a white velvet box on the table. "Your jewels. Shall I send for the fitter now, or would mademoiselle have her bath first?"

"I—" Britt shrugged helplessly. "The fitter first, please."

When the girl had gone, Britt took up the velvet case and opened it. Inside lay an emerald necklace so startlingly beautiful against the white cloth, that she gasped. Paste, of course, and imitation diamonds in the clasp, but how skillfully made! How dazzlingly magnificent.

With trembling fingers she lifted the necklace from the box and laid it against her creamy throat. The green stones picked up the color of her eyes at once and set a sparkle in them that hadn't been present since the day Philippe had put her on the train in Limoges.

Who had supplied such splendor, she wondered, turning again to gaze admiringly at the dress, its deep rich pile of velvet all but glowing? Surely not Margo! This room she could credit to her, thought Britt, with a grim little smile, but not velvet and emeralds.

Martinique, then. She was the one, of course. How

dear of her! Philippe's aunt must have guessed how
sorely in need her reporter friend would be of some
little bit of glamor on this most bitter of nights. Margo
had said Britt's feelings for Philippe were written all
over her face. Martinique must have read them there
and taken pity on her.

Whatever the reason, she thought, gratefully bringing one soft sleeve to her cheek, the assurance that she
would appear at the ball as elegantly attired as the
wealthiest guest bolstered her faltering spirits, and by
the time the fitter arrived, Britt found she was able to
greet her with a smile and to lend a willing ear to the
seamstress's gossipy chatter concerning the ball.

Britt discovered, however, that making her entrance
into the empty ballroom a few minutes before the
guests were due to assemble was quite a different
matter from turning slowly in her velvet dress before
the approving eyes of a dressmaker.

The ballroom was immense, the decorations overpowering in the medieval grandeur they reproduced.
The hushed expectancy that held the room gripped
Britt as well, and she stood trembling in the doorway,
aware that she should be shooting her photographs
before the hordes of guests in their billowing costumes
blotted out the setting. But still she stood transfixed.

Margo had outdone herself. If this was any indication
of the kind of hostess she would make for the Chateau
de Laon, then no doubt Philippe was proud of her.
Every detail was perfect.

"Ah. Here you are."

Britt turned. Philippe! He had come soundlessly into
the room, dressed for the ball, the "very perfect, gentle
Knight" of Chaucer's tale, slim, broad-shouldered and
dark, his sensuous mouth curved in a half-smile, his

voice low and disturbingly resonant. "I've been looking for you."

When Britt could trust her own voice, she replied coldly, "Did you think I'd dare disobey your command to appear?"

A subtle change occurred in his eyes. "Would you have come if I hadn't commanded?"

"Certainly not!"

His shoulders lifted slightly. "I thought as much."

"Why should I?" she retorted. "I've no business here."

"It seems you have." His gaze went to the camera in her hand. "I'm glad to see you've recovered the tool of your trade."

Blood raced to her cheeks.

She was dressed in the same finery as his guests, but she was not a guest. The camera marked her. All evening, according to his plan for humiliating her, she would have to carry it, shattering the soft glow of torches with garish bursts from her flashbulbs. She was to be the incongruous element, the out-of-place twentieth century element in this ancient setting, as out-of-place as she had always been in the life of Philippe Dolman. This was what he had fetched her here to tell her in the cruelest way he could.

Her voice came out a whisper in the silent ballroom. "I despise you."

He regarded her solemnly. "You think I've betrayed you."

"You've done worse than that. You've forced me into the dust, and now you're grinding your heel on me. Does it make you happy?" Her eyes glittered with unshed tears. "Does it give you pleasure?"

"To see you here?" His glance moved over her. "The greatest pleasure imaginable."

"You've chosen your bride well," she choked. "You deserve each other."

"I hope so," he answered quietly. "I expect to be supremely happy with her, and it's my fondest hope that she will be happy with me as well."

"She will, I'm sure, with the chateau as her home," Britt flung at him.

"And the farm."

Britt flinched. The farm, the dearest place in all the world to her. He was even more cruel than she had imagined! Her heart ached so she could scarcely breathe. "If you'll excuse me, I have work to do."

"Not now," he answered, and before she was aware of what he was doing, he had taken the camera from her.

"But it has to be now! In a few minutes the room will be so crowded I won't be able to get a clear shot of the decorations."

"It doesn't matter."

Britt's eyes blazed. "I see! You've forced me down here, but you won't let me do my job now that I'm here. That's your scheme, is it? You want me to go back to Paris empty-handed so you can ruin the magazine." She had gone the color of chalk. "Oh, you do a thing up to perfection once you set your teeth to it, don't you, Monsieur Dolman!"

"Not always." A muscle rippled in his cheek. "But this time—" His nostrils flared. "This time nothing less than perfection will do."

"Britt, my dear!" Martinique, a well-rounded cream puff in gold satin, descended upon them. "How beautiful you look!" She planted a kiss on Britt's pale cheek. "I'm so glad to see you. And the color of your gown, my dear. It couldn't be more perfect."

"Thanks to you," said Britt stiffly. "Now if I can have my camera, please—"

"Camera?" Martinique frowned. "Oh no, my dear. Not tonight. Philippe?" She turned to verify her objections with her nephew, but Philippe, camera in hand, was halfway across the ballroom.

Chapter 21

Britt stood seething in the shadows of the ballroom entrance while the guests in their magnificent costumes arranged themselves for the Grand March which would officially begin the ball.

Without her camera, she was not a photographer hired for the occasion, and without an escort, she was not a member of the bejeweled body of revelers surrounding her. She had no role at all. Philippe was a monster!

Trembling with rage, she watched as he made his way through the crowd and took his place beside Margo at its head. The orchestra struck the first note of the march, and the dazzling spectacle began.

Margo, her golden tresses arranged in a towering coil, was radiant in miles of white satin and lace. What would she choose for her wedding gown? Britt wondered. Anything less elegant than her present attire would be an anticlimax, and anything more elegant would tax the imagination of even the most skilled designer. How ironic, Britt thought with a stab of malicious satisfaction, if the bride upstaged herself at her own engagement party!

But Britt's brief indulgence in vindictiveness was short-lived. Even she had to admit that the dark-haired Philippe in burnished waistcoat and close-fitting trousers cut to follow the lean tautness of his thighs and muscled calves made the perfect counterpart for Margo's glowing blondeness. They were a strikingly handsome couple, and the waves of admiration that rippled over the crowded ballroom as they made their way across it, attested to the fact that everyone there regarded them as a storybook couple.

Had Britt been alone, she would have turned and fled. But just as the music had begun, she had felt a soft hand upon her arm and turning, discovered she had been joined by Martinique. Now the older woman clung to her, starry-eyed, while the intricate pattern of the march evolved.

"Isn't it magnificent?" Martinique breathed.

"Stunning," Britt managed. Just what *La Revue* had sent her here to photograph, she thought bitterly. Now what would happen to Sydney's job? How could she ever explain Philippe's ruthless behavior?

Once more Philippe and Margo, who had circled the entire room, appeared almost within touching distance. Philippe's dark eyes sought out Britt's brimming ones, and she looked quickly away. This was beyond endurance!

"You must excuse me," she murmured, pulling away from Martinique, but the older woman only gripped her arm more firmly.

"The most beautiful part is about to begin. You mustn't miss it."

"Let me go, please!"

But Martinique seemed completely oblivious to Britt's agony. "Look! Philippe is giving the signal for the music to stop. He's going to make the announcement."

When the orchestra stopped playing, the great hall became still at once. Philippe mounted a turreted cupola affixed to a center supporting column and began to speak.

"Ladies and gentlemen, honored guests. Ordinarily on occasions of this sort if there are announcements to be made, they come at the stroke of midnight. They are the high point of the evening toward which all the rest is directed."

He paused a moment and leveled a gaze on Margo. "But it is my desire tonight that you should all be aware from the start of the joyous circumstances which inspired this ball so that we might celebrate together throughout the evening."

Not a whisper broke the hush of the hall. Britt wondered if even Martinique would notice if she crumpled in a faint. *Philippe and Margo.* Days ago she had faced the truth of their forthcoming marriage, but now that the moment for the announcement of it had arrived, she could not bear the pain of it. Philippe lost forever. What point was there in living?

Philippe's voice rang out again. "In addition, let it be known that our joy here tonight is two-fold." He took Margo's hand in his and lifted it.

"First," he said, "may I present to you Margo of the house of St. Croix. The much beloved ward of my late father, and since his death, my ward."

Through tear-blurred eyes, Britt saw Margo step forward and bow in a low-sweeping curtsy. She saw the dazzling smile that brought gasps of admiration from the thrilled onlookers. There was no mistaking that Margo was beauteous almost beyond belief—and equally as cruel and selfish. She would destroy Philippe.

Suddenly to Britt this was the most difficult part of all to bear. Was there nothing she could do to stop their marriage? Could she cry out now? Make a devastating scene? Create havoc on the night of Margo's triumph? What would Philippe do? Would he marry her anyway?

Philippe spoke again. "You are present here tonight as witnesses to the coming of age of Mademoiselle St. Croix, who after this evening will assume her new role as mistress of her family's ancestral estate on the island of St. Croix in the Carribean Sea."

"And who invites each of you," Margo took up in a clear voice, "to come and visit there whenever you can."

Cheers filled the ballroom. Britt's dazed stare fixed itself on Margo's radiant smile as she received the congratulations of her friends. At Britt's elbow, Martinique murmured, "Half a world away. It's scarcely far enough, is it?"

"But St. Croix—" Britt's reply came in a stranger's voice. "What does it mean? Is it to be a summer home for the two of them?"

Martinique was saved from answering by Philippe's hands raised again for silence. "And now you must hear our other reason for celebration."

The cheers died down. Britt felt the room spin. *This is it. Now the world will know, and my world will end.*

Philippe's resonant voice reached out to every corner of the vast, silent room. "The occasion of my distant cousin Margo's assumption of inheritance," he said in a dramatic cadence, "serves also to mark the announcement of a soon-to-be assumption of my own." There was a split-second pause. "The taking to myself of a wife."

A unanimous intake of breath split the charged

atmosphere. Philippe's grave face broke into a smile. "It is my very great privilege and pleasure and joy to present to you now my bride-to-be, late of Land's End and the future mistress of the Chateau de Laon— Mademoiselle Britt Ryan."

In an instant, the cheering crowd parted, and Britt in a state of shock saw Philippe striding toward her.

"Oh, my dear girl!" Martinique gasped breathlessly at her elbow. "I can't tell you how overjoyed I am."

Then Philippe was beside her, and with an arm encircling her waist, he led her swiftly back to the center of the room.

Numbly she watched as dozens of costumed waiters appeared out of nowhere bearing trays of sparkling crystal glasses filled with champagne. Edouard Rimbaud stepped forward from the crowd and proposed the toast, which was greeted with more cheers and thunderous applause and heartily drunk to amid much laughter and the joyous clinking of the fragile stemware.

Britt, still stunned, stared blankly up at Philippe. "I'm dreaming. That must be it."

He pulled her close. "Yes, my darling," he answered thickly. "But it's the dream of a lifetime, and one, thank God, from which neither of us need ever awaken."

"You took a terrible chance, you know."

Britt, speaking in the dawn light filtering into the garden room where Philippe held her in his arms, nestled closer to the heartbeat that was as vital to her as her own. "I might have said 'no' right there in front of all your friends."

"I wouldn't have blamed you if you had," Philippe murmured into her hair. "But I would have gone straight out and shot myself."

"Your friends' opinions of you matter so much?" she teased gently.

"Nothing matters but you. Tell me why in heaven's name it took me so long to discover that."

"There were complications," she answered lightly. And then in a more serious tone, "Don't you think it's time you explained how they were finally resolved?"

His lips moved on her cheek. "I'd rather kiss you again," which he proceeded to do with a passion that sent a spasm of longing up her spine. Reluctantly she broke free and pulled him toward the window seat. "Come. Sit down and tell me. I've been patient all evening."

He chuckled. "I thought you were being joyous and carefree and saucy and wonderful—but patient? That never showed once."

"That's only because you were so busy making me happy you didn't notice." Then unable to resist his nearness, she lifted her lips again for his kiss.

For a long while in the strengthening light of the dawn he held her, his hands moving possessively over the curves of her slender body and returning to frame the pixie face he had first glimpsed from his balloon.

"The maid from the meadow," he murmured hoarsely. "My lovely Britt."

"When can we go up again?" she whispered against his throat.

"In the balloon?" he sighed. "Winter's coming on, but maybe the gods will grant us one more day of perfect winds." His lips found the soft underside of her earlobe. "But I'm more interested in our wedding day."

Britt took a deep breath. "What beautiful words. I'd given up all hope of ever hearing them."

"Did you think me a terrible brute that day at the farmhouse?"

"Yes, and when Sydney told me you were forcing the magazine to send me here to cover the ball, I hated you." She paused. "But then—"

"Go on—it's our night for confessions."

"Then I saw you from my window overlooking the garden, and I knew I'd always love you no matter what you did."

His arms closed around her. "The same thing happened to me when you drove away from the farm that day."

"I've wondered," she said. "What did happen after I left?"

"I couldn't bear the sight of Margo so I walked in the orchard. Then I went back down to the river where you and I sailed in the punt. I spent some time in that little barn where we were sheltered from the rain." He lifted her chin and met the glow in her eyes. "You were in all those places, Britt. Everywhere I looked, I saw you. I felt as if some part of me had gone away with you, and I felt—" He hesitated. "I hoped and prayed after a while it might draw you back to me."

"I would never have come back on my own accord."

"I realized that. Then I went back to the house. Margo was furious. When the Rimbauds, tactful as always, left us to ourselves, she lit into me for all she was worth. I let her voice all her threats again, and then I told her I didn't care what she did."

"But you did care!"

He shook his head. "No—only about you. I told Margo she could charge me in court or not, as she pleased. She could spread her filthy lies in every newspaper on the Continent if she liked, but I would never marry her, not under any circumstance."

"Philippe, how could you risk that? You love the chateau so."

"I love you more. I nearly lost you before I discovered that losing anything else was meaningless in comparison."

They kissed again, fresh wonder at the power of love enfolding Britt anew.

When they parted, Britt said, "But I still don't understand what made Margo change her mind." She started suddenly. "She isn't— She wouldn't!"

"Go ahead with her plan?" His arm tightened about her reassuringly. "No, no. There'd have been no ball tonight if that had been the case. She agreed two days ago to drop all threats. Then the only remaining problem was how to persuade you to return to me."

But Britt was still puzzling over Margo's about-face. "You still haven't told me what caused Margo to change her mind. You must have discovered a powerful weapon of your own to use against her."

He shook his head. "For one thing, the sport went out of her challenge when she was convinced that I meant what I said—that I'd never give in to her."

He took a breath. "But the main reason she capitulated was the one you thought of when she first threatened us. Margo's ruthless, but she's clever too, and as you guessed, when she added up the odds, she realized she'd be damaged as much as I by any allegations she took to court. If only I'd acted more quickly. Think what could have been saved."

Britt nestled closer. "But think what I would have missed tonight. That lovely ball in my honor." She ran her hand over the velvet of her skirt. "This most beautiful of dresses."

"You haven't mentioned the necklace."

Her fingers went to it. "It's magnificent."

"It's your engagement gift." Then he added casually, "It was given first to Eugenie Monserrat three hundred years ago. Every Dolman bride since has worn it."

Britt sat up straight. "Do you mean it's real? These stones are really emeralds? These are diamonds?"

He laughed. "Of course."

"Oh, Philippe! I had no idea. I thought—" She ran the tip of her tongue across her lips. "Paste, that's what I thought. And glass."

"But do you like it?"

She fell back limply. "How could I not? Even when I thought it was only costume jewelry I loved it." A dismayed look controlled her delicate features. "Oh, Philippe, I don't belong here. I can't be mistress of the Chateau de Laon. Diamonds and emeralds appear the same to me as paste and glass. I'm too ordinary a person to fit into your life. Why, this necklace is worth more than my father could have earned in two lifetimes. I haven't the grace or the appreciation or any of the attributes you must have in a wife. I'll be an eternal embarrassment to you."

"Do you love me?" he said quietly.

She came swiftly into his arms. "You know I do. I have for so long that nothing which happened before I loved you seems to have any reality at all."

His fingers moved through the black tendrils curling at the nape of her neck. "Then you're all I'll ever need or want in a wife, my darling."

"There aren't any words I'd rather hear," she cried, "but love won't make me a gracious hostess. I'll make no end of blunders. This one with the necklace is only the first."

"You lectured me on love once," he answered with a bemused smile. "You told me love has a life of its own apart from the flesh—" He paused, searching his memory for the words. "Apart from the vagaries of the senses, you said. Now let me add to your definition: love can surmount all obstacles." He kissed her.

"You've made a believer out of me and nothing can move me now from that belief. Together we can overcome everything." His lips found hers again. "Tell me you have that kind of faith too, Britt."

"I want to," she whispered. "I can't live without you."

"Nor I without you. Besides," he teased, "you plighted me your troth tonight before those hundreds of persons. You can't renege now."

"I don't want to! But I'm afraid, Philippe."

He pulled her against his chest. "We haven't room in our lives for fear, Britt. Fear cripples. We're free to live in this world, you and I, and we're going to live gloriously. If problems arise, we can solve them together."

She sighed. "You make it sound so easy."

"It is actually. Think. Twenty-four hours ago would you have dreamed we'd be here together planning our future?"

"Never."

"Then you see? Anything is possible. Believe that. Believe in me."

Britt felt her doubts slipping from her as Philippe's arms wrapped her more closely. "Oh, darling, I do love you. But tell me," she said after a moment. "Margo—is she happy?"

"As happy as she's capable of being, I suppose," Philippe answered.

"I can't believe she's leaving France. What about all her friends, the social life she values so highly?"

"She'll still have it, only on a grander scale. She'll be an international socialite, and nothing could please her more. The estate in St. Croix is really a palace. I never cared for living there, so it was no great wrench for me to deed the place to her. Probably she'll spend half the year there entertaining; then the other half on the

Continent letting her friends repay her courtesies. It's exactly the kind of life she's suited for."

"So you did have to bribe her a little," said Britt, making an effort not to sound too disappointed.

"Not at all," Philippe replied crisply. "I didn't tell her until tonight just before the ball that I was giving her the castle. My only prior concession was allowing her to be present for the masquerade, and I thought that only fair since it was she who planned the whole thing."

"She knew you were going to announce our engagement?"

"Certainly. I told Martinique too." He squeezed her hand. "I had to have someone stand guard over you in case at the last minute you decided to bolt."

"I tried to. You were a devil to take away my camera."

He laughed. "I couldn't very well lead my fiancée to the fore bearing that thing, could I?"

"You ought to have had to!" she replied indignantly. "Making such a fuss at *La Revue*. Poor Sydney almost suffered a relapse. And what's he to do now? Not a single picture was taken at the ball."

"That's just as it should be," said Philippe with a contented sigh. "Once upon a time I let a photographer into my home and see what came of it. Never again!"

Britt smiled. "I don't care if I never see another camera, but that doesn't help poor Sydney. He was furious that I didn't get you to sign the release. What if he loses his job?"

"Don't worry. The moment I was notified you'd arrived at the chateau, I sent word to *La Revue* that the whole mixup had been settled to my complete satisfaction and that the release would be in tomorrow's mail. You can rest assured everyone is happy in Paris this morning."

Laughter from a late group of revelers drifted in from the hallway.

"Everyone's happy here, too." Britt lifted a contented face to Philippe's luminous gaze. "Most especially Philippe of the house of Dolman and plain Britt Ryan, late of Land's End."